The *Yellow Rose*

A Novel Of The Texas Revolution

Bob Stewart & Carl R. Brush

BOOKSIDE Press

BookSide Press
877-741-8091
www.booksidepress.com
orders@booksidepress.com

CONTENTS

The Yellow Rose, is a tale set during the Texas Revolution of 1836. It mixes legend with fact. No one knows whether our Emily West met Sam Houston or if she participated in the revolution at all. On the other hand, no one has proved the contrary. *The Yellow Rose* asks the question: What if . . .

CHAPTER ONE

A Legend Begins— February 24, 1836

"Girl, let's have another." He waved his mug at the end of a buckskin-clad arm, fringe dancing under an armpit stained with sweat, and smelling, I'm sure, worse than a dead polecat. Sure as cotton's white, though, I wasn't about to test that surmise.

They called me "girl" a lot in that saloon, but somehow my skin didn't crawl when Sam Houston said it. He didn't use the derogatory tone most of these louts did with us dark people. I could slough off that sort of thing better than most, being that I'm a high yellow mix of white and black, hair that curls with nary a kink, plus I'm not the slave they figured me for. But that constant "boy" "girl" "boy" "girl" business still felt like needles jabbing, jabbing, jabbing all the time. Houston, though, he sounded like he was just calling for service, beginning, middle and end of it. That's what got me interested in the first place. I nodded in his direction and made my way toward him, dodging and slapping away the customary pats and squeezes on the rear—and higher. The clients of the Morgan's Point Hotel saloon were rougher than an outhouse corncob.

"That's what I like," Houston spoke to his companions without taking his eyes off me, "a woman who steps right to it when a man calls."

"What say, General?" said the man sitting across the table from him.

"Turn your good ear so you can hear me, Deef," Houston said to him. Then, playing to rest of the table, he yelled, "Oh, I forgot, Deef ain't got a good ear."

The men roared their delight, the man called Deef right along with them.

He wasn't much to look at, this Sam Houston. Nose a bit too big, lips too thin, his hairline headed north. Kind of disappointing, since I'd heard so much about what a warrior he was. Wounded hero of the Battle of New Orleans, where he impressed General Andrew Jackson. President Andrew Jackson now. And the gossip here is Old Hickory sent him to Galveston Bay several years ago to pull this godforsaken Mexican hot box into the Union. Why? It didn't seem to me it was worth the wind it'd take to blow every grain of sand of it into the Gulf, which seemed likely to happen any day. He just wanted to prove he could do it was my guess. Like any man. Seems like what makes the most sense is just leave it to the Mexicans. But nobody asked me. Nobody ever does.

Houston and his buddies were on their way to getting glassy-eyed but hadn't quite arrived there yet. I made sure Houston got a glimpse of what's inside my low-necked bodice when I bent over to pick up his mug. When I had his attention, I turned around, gave my hips an extra sway, and tossed a smile and a wink back over my shoulder on my way back to the bar. I felt his lust. Good. Bigger tips meant bigger savings.

On my return trip, I renegotiated that gauntlet of eager hands, then plopped the brew in front of him, directing a bit of a splash down his front in the process. Why, I don't know. To remember me by, I suppose.

"What the hell?" He jumped to his feet and bellowed like a cow calling her calf.

"Sorry I got your dirty clothes clean," I said, mopping at the suds foaming on his matted chest hair.

"Leave it," he said, slapping my hands away.

I was surprised to discover I had to lift up my chin to look in his eyes. Most men I look at straight across, and a goodly number have to lift their eyes to meet mine. Houston wasn't ten feet tall like the stories said, but he had me by a good three or four inches. Maybe I hadn't given him enough credit at first glance.

Still and all, he didn't look like someone you'd count on to turn a mismatched conglomeration of Anglos, blacks, and Mexicans into an army fit to throw off the likes of General Santa Anna. Quite a gamble for Old Hickory to back him. Like betting on a long shot in a cock fight. But maybe the president did that, too.

Houston's watery blue eyes scanned me. He tilted his head like a dog, curious and wary about a cat he's happened on. He swayed a bit. Not unusual for our patrons this time of night, but more noticeable with his height.

"You're a tall one," he said.

"Is that what makes you a great leader?" I said. "Your knack for spotting what's obvious?"

"Here, girl, keep your mouth to yourself." A coarse voice flared behind me, a rough hand grasped a fistful of my sleeve and pulled me back.

Houston laughed and held up a hand as the man I would come to know as Deef Smith pulled me back. I was about to treat Deef's hand to a taste of my fingernails when Houston said, "No, Deef. Leave her be. She's got gumption, and you know I like a good laugh." He reached to dislodge his buddy's hand but never took his eyes off me the whole time, nor did I take mine off his. I felt Deef release his grip and retreat. Big dog, little dog. I'd seen this act before.

"He hears better than he makes out, doesn't he?" I said.

"You don't speak like a southern nigger," Houston said.

"Nossuh," I said, mimicking the accent of a southern chattel. "I's from New Yohk."

"Then why are you here?"

"Mr. Morgan signed me on to look out for his warehouse and serve here in his saloon."

"Signed you on? Contract, then?"

"One year," I said, "and with six months to go, I wish it was over."

"So you're a free one, are you?"

"Cross my heart." I batted my eyelashes and patted the place under my blouse where I had my papers tucked away. "Lots more of us around than you might want to think."

"Warehouse. Big job for a man like Jim Morgan to trust to a girl, free or not. So must be you can read and write and cypher."

"Me?" I said, simpering and looking up at him with half-closed eyes, "a simple bar girl?"

Houston smiled. "Deef," he said, sitting back down and grasping the handle of his mug, "we must treat this woman with respect. She's probably more educated than you and me."

"That's a safe bet," I said

He stuck out his hand. "Houston's the name. Sam Houston."

I didn't take his hand immediately. "I don't have to read, write or cypher to know who you are, General."

He didn't withdraw his hand. "It's Sam to you Miss … " He raised his eyebrows.

I finally deigned to clasp his hand. "West. Emily, General Houston."

"Well, West. Emily. Would you draw me a bath and see to my buckskins? He lifted a pair of saddlebags from the floor and slapped them on the table. "I have another outfit in here needs washing as well."

'I'll draw your bath, General," I said. Then I whispered, "and that's all."

"What did you say, girl?" Deef said.

Houston shrugged. "Deef, here, didn't catch that, but I heard you loud and clear."

Deef nodded and Houston downed his beer and marched off toward the stairs that led to the upstairs rooms. I gathered the saddlebags and followed, Deef straggling behind me.

My mind was racing. I'd thought I had control of the situation with this overgrown, half-drunk, so-called general, and then suddenly I was left holding his dusty saddlebags and chasing him up the stairs. My first lesson in how quickly Sam Houston could turn the tables in his favor.

CHAPTER TWO

The Bath

With his long legs, even unsteady as he was, he gained several steps on me over the course of the dozen stairs and short hallway that led to his room. He entered ahead, left the door open, and Deef, close behind me, hollered before proceeding to his own room next door, "Let me know if you need anything, General." He paused to throw me a poison look. I smiled back, winked. He looked like he was about to spit at me, but he didn't. Just stomped into the room and slammed the door.

I passed over the General's threshold and closed his door behind me. He stood by the copper tub with his back to me, in the process of disrobing.

He said without looking at me, "Once you've pulled out those filthy duds, just toss the saddlebags on the bed."

I did what he asked—"commanded" would be a better word. Under the dirty clothes, I noticed a plump bag of what looked like coins. Was he trusting, forgetful, or testing me? Whatever the case, I knew enough to let it be. Then I stepped toward the fireplace where a pot filled with water hung heating up over the flames. This was the most luxurious room in Mr. Morgan's Hotel—The Brazos Suite. In New York they'd have laughed the week away at the idea of calling a single room a suite, but this had its own fireplace, which put it at the top of the frontier heap. If Deef Smith, for example, wanted to get clean—a big if—he'd have to go down the street to the common bathhouse and plunk himself into a tub in the presence of a half-dozen other filthy creatures.

"I'll just leave these here for you to take care of," he said as he let his pants slide to the floor and swung one long leg into the tub, one hand out to brace himself.

I almost remarked it was a strange way to show me the respect he'd talked about downstairs to bare himself like I was a common whore. But I heard my mother's voice in my head and bit my saucy tongue. I may have been a free woman, but I was still a servant and a long ways from home. Just February to October till my year was up and I'd get my pay and my passage east and this outpost nightmare would be over. Right now, though, the only difference between me and a slave was that my servitude had a time limit. I couldn't afford to cross Mr. Morgan till I was back with my mother in his Hudson River summer house. What Morgan was paying me, combined with her savings and my tips would be enough to get us out of service and into the inn-keeping business we'd dreamt about for years.

But I couldn't quite leave things be. I slid back into my slave dialect. I said, "I'se comin' directly with yoh bath water, Gen'rul, suh."

He just sat there humming and drumming his dirty fingers on the sides of the tub. Soon the humming stopped, his eyes closed, and he drifted off. I won't say he passed out, though that might be nearer the truth. I picked up the hooked rod, tipped the steaming pot, and filled the bucket that had been waiting on the hearth. It had been a wet, cold year in Point Morgan. Unusually so from what the locals said, so the roof tank was full. Otherwise, Bayard, our scullery boy— forty years old and still a boy, you understand—Bayard would have had fill these pots bucket by bucket, struggling his way up the stairs from the back yard pump to do it. As it was, there was a spout from the roof tank in the hallway, and Bayard had a fairly easy task to keep the pots filled and the fire stoked.

"Here it comes, General," I said as I approached the tub. "Fair warning, it's a little warm."

Houston's eyelids flew open, but he didn't respond otherwise. I smiled to myself as I lifted the bucket. Normally, I'd ask the gentleman to cover himself, then pour the first bucket slowly from the foot of the tub to give him time to get used to the temperature. However, Houston had already proved disinclined toward modesty, so I marched right to the center of the tub, then stopped. An ugly wound on his right shoulder leaked a bit of pus.

"Did you get that injury fighting with indians or against them?"

It was none of my affair, but everyone knew he'd spent some time with the Cherokees in Carolina or Tennessee or some such place. Maybe even had a wife or two there. Some said he was trying to get some local chief named Bowl—a name so comical for an Indian chief I figured it was made up—to side with him against the Mexicans.

"One way or the other, I suppose," he mumbled.

So he wanted me to shut up about it. Nothing is more sure to make me keep a conversation going. "When?"

"'Bout, I don't know how long ago. Some Indian war leading up to the battle of New Orleans, or maybe in that battle."

I felt a budding compassion for the man. That was nearly two dozen years ago. The wound sure looked fresh, more like an injury that required immediate nursing than one that was years old. Was he lying? I couldn't think of a reason why he would.

"Would you like for me to tend it for you?"

"Girl, I been tending it for years."

It sounded like my kindness not only counted for nothing, but even annoyed him. That infuriated me. I'd stop that smart mouth. I aimed at a spot some inches below his belly button and dumped the whole bucket in one hot waterfall. I was gratified to see his lobster turn pink and jump out of its nest.

"How's the temperature, General?" I asked. I tried to keep my tone businesslike, but I was inwardly giggling that I'd revenged myself for his earlier insolence. His little man would be tender for a while. Give him credit though. Most men would have jumped up in a rage, but Houston didn't flinch.

"Perfect, girl," he said. "Keep it coming." This time, the way he said "girl" carried the same insulting tone the rest of the men used. So, what had started as a friendly relationship had turned hostile. I was surprised I felt disappointed, since there was no possible future to him and me, but I was satisfied that I'd made my point without getting into an argument that would have gotten back to Mr. Morgan. Only problem was, I might have compromised my tip. Oh, well, the show was well worth the price of admission. But, I couldn't say it was no little thing.

I finished filling the tub, placed the basket with towels and bars of soap on the stool beside it. I scooped up the dirty clothes, caught a glimpse of that poke of money, and got myself an idea. I'd need to think on it to decide whether it was a good idea or a bad one. For the moment, I just asked if there was anything else he needed. By that time, he'd slid down so that he was nearly underwater.

"A beer and a girl," he said. Then he pushed himself up, water streaming down his shoulders, turned to me and smiled. "Not you, Emily West, of course." Then he slid back underwater.

Was that an apology? A truce? Or did it mean nothing at all?

I dropped him a curtsy, playing the southern belle now. "I declay-uh, General. You ah the veruh soul of chivalry."

CHAPTER THREE

Watching Emily— February 25, 1836

Deef Smith swung the iron pot from over the fire, dropped a couple of eggshells into the cowboy coffee, then dipped in two tin cups.

"Just let them float. They'll sink eventually," I said.

Erastus chuckled and shook his head. "How long I've knowed you General? Three? Four years? Maybe more? And you say the same thing every mornin'."

"And you laugh."

Erastus nodded, a grinned creasing his salt and pepper beard. He had lost two thirds of his hearing in a childhood illness and was immediately tagged Deef by the Anglos or El Sordo by the Mexicans, but I had trouble thinking of him as Deef, someone less than whole. Before putting the steaming cups on the table at my elbow, he used a spoon to dip out the floating eggshells he always insisted on dropping into the boiling pot.

"Settles the grounds," he said in a high-pitched voice, almost a monotone. He put the cups on the table then pulled up a chair to join me. I nodded.

"You don't have to always say that."

"What?"

"Turn your good ear toward me."

"You don't have to shout, General. I can hear you, read your lips if I have to."

"And you don't have to always tell me about the eggshells."

He turned sullen and nodded, looking out the window.

"They're about loaded." He nodded, taking a sip of the bitter brew and scowling. "That's fine coffee."

Outside, Emily West stepped into view and my groin responded, not in delight, but to the memory of the burning pitcher of water she'd poured into the tub last night. I wanted children some day. Hoped she hadn't spoiled my plans. Still, I chuckled. Erastus' head swung around, eyes furrowed in question.

"I don't think you're as deaf as they say, Mr. Deef Smith."

"My good ear," he said, grinning back and shaking a head of wild red curls.

"She's a right smart pretty woman," Erastus said. "Probably her breeding, from New York, just like me. And smart enough to come to Texas, just like me. But she sure is a bit uppity for a nigger."

I nodded. "I'm not sure she's here because she wants to be. I understand she's Dr. Morgan's slave, although she claims not to be."

Erastus continued. "Gossip is she was a free woman who gave up a year's freedom to indenture to Morgan to buy some house in the Hudson Valley that belonged to her Daddy. She ain't no whore, but they's her friends."

A man jumped into one of the freight wagons and pried up most of the flooring.

"Don't you think it strange that she can read and write and cipher?"

"Never gave it no mind. But, yeah, you're right 'bout that. I can read a bit, cypher in my head enough so no barkeep cheats me, but I still sign an 'X', like I did when I signed up for your army. You'd be surprised what people say in front of the deef and dumb, General."

"Erastus. I know you heard me, before. It's not *my* army, it's the army of the people of Texas. And I'm not general until the constitution is written and the powers that be say so."

"Then why you got that brand-new uniform in N'awlins?"

"Just in case. I sure won't turn it down if it's offered and I expect it to be."

This topic made me uneasy. I came to Texas because President Jackson sent me to help bring it into the union. Andy Jackson would prefer slave, and we are far enough south for that to happen. But we are a long ways west, and it's doubtful what will happen in that direction. Either way, my job is to get rid of Santa Anna and everything else will follow. After living here a few years, it was easy to understand why. The countryside is the most beautiful I've ever seen and there's enough lumber in pine forests to build every house in America. There's a fortune to be made here. Only thing is, there's a Mexican tyrant and his army in the way. We just need to throw off Mexican oppression and free the people. It'd be my job to take care of the Mexicans. The people would take care of everything else.

CHAPTER FOUR

Loading Up

I could feel Houston watching from the hotel window. I told myself it wasn't just me, that he had plenty of reason to be interested in this convoy. The constitutional convention which was about to commence at Washington-on-the-Brazos needed the liquor to fuel the negotiations and the guns to fuel the revolution that would follow. I knew well which window was his room, and it was easy to see, even through the mist and drizzle, that he and Deef Smith were standing there, and since I was the only woman—at least the only one in charge of anything—involved in loading these wagons, they couldn't help but notice. And … I told myself once again to quit jumping to conclusions. It would be quite enough good fortune for Houston not to notice me or the hefty addition I'd made to his bundle of laundry before I'd returned it this morning; Namely, a purse containing my savings from my labors at the the resort. I figured it was tit-for-tat for the money he'd left in plain sight as a test of my honesty on the night of the bath. I figured it would be safer with him than anyplace I could leave it at the resort or carry on the wagon train. Not till I was well on the road, anyway. I turned my attention back to the job at hand.

The way we did those wagons reminded me of baking cakes in my mother's kitchen. First the men were going to place a layer of weapons and ammunition, then new floorboards like icing, then a layer of whisky barrels and beer on the top, then a tarpaulin for frosting.

The trip would take a good four days through some wild country, and there were plenty of bandidos and Indians roaming the hills, not to mention General Santa Anna's troops. If we were attacked, the idea was they'd be satisfied with the alcohol and miss the false bottom, and General Houston's troops would still get their arms. It seemed a flimsy plan to me, but I wasn't in charge.

The rifles weren't flintlocks. U.S. Common Rifles they were called, and they used percussion caps with a paper cartridge and a greased ball. Faster loading than the muzzle loaders and not so vulnerable to the weather. The pistols were brand-new Colt revolvers. Strange looking compared to the curved-handle style I was used to. The men were surprised I was interested in the details of what they were lifting out of the crates and on to the wagons. I told them I was in charge of warehouses and had gotten used to matching bills of lading to merchandise. Men are always surprised when women want to know about business or mechanics or anything they don't consider female concerns. I never get tired of surprising them or even offending them with my curiosity. Another thing I was curious about was where the money for these modern armaments came from. I knew better than to ask these gentlemen about that, but maybe I'd get a chance to put the question to Houston one of these days.

"You're overloading that wagon," I called to a couple of teamsters. "You get into sand or mud and the mules won't be able to move it."

A red-bearded stick of a man who looked like he'd have a hard time boosting a feather pillow, let alone the whisky barrel he'd just lifted into the wagon bed, turned and snarled at me. "That happens, we'll just hitch up a second team to it." He spat tobacco juice not quite at me after he said it. "You show me you can handle a team, you can start giving me orders."

"My name's Miss West," I said. "What's yours?"

"Jake," he said.

"Glad to meet you," I said. Neither of us offered to shake hands. "I'd appreciate it if you'd just wait here a minute."

I'd been through this before, but Jake apparently hadn't gotten the word. I didn't mind proving myself. It broke up the monotony. There were three wagons waiting in line to be loaded. I walked back to the second in line just to make the short trip a little more difficult. I untied the reins from the log on the uphill side of the road, hoisted myself up to the wagon seat, picked up the whip, and released the brake lever. The road wasn't wide enough for two wagons, so I had to swing out on the downslope to get around the one in front of me. Nothing too dangerous, even with the ground a bit muddy and slippery, but it was a navigation problem a novice driver would have had trouble with. The team could get going downhill, and if you couldn't stop them you'd pile up. Or if you turned them too sharp while you were gaining momentum, you might jackknife. A mess either way.

"Haw," I yelled as I pulled the four mules to the left and cracked the whip in the air. Dr. Morgan had taught me to put a growl on when I gave commands because the animals weren't used to obeying a woman's voice. We got downslope a ways, and I pulled the reins the other way, growled, "gee," gave the whip another crack and pulled up smoothly behind the wagon Jake had been loading. I told him that his wagon was full and to get going loading this one. Then I jumped down and walked past him to look to other matters.

He called after me. "We ain't going to get all them other barrels in just these here wagons."

I turned. "Probably not," I said. "But overloaded wagons will never make it to Washington-on-the-Brazos. I'm told more wagons are on the way, but even if they don't arrive, better to leave some supplies here than to have to jettison them in the wilds."

Jake spat again, but this time he turned away from me to do it.

I walked away from him toward the lead wagon in the train. It was nearing time to leave, and I needed to inspect all the tack and trees before we pulled out.

While I walked, I glanced back to Houston's window. Smith continued to watch intently, the general had disappeared. Well, he wasn't my responsibility any longer. My job now was to prepare Dr. Morgan's wagons for the trip from here to the constitutional convention. If we didn't make it there in good shape, the package I'd left with Sam Houston would be in jeopardy. Whatever else was going to happen with him would take care of itself.

CHAPTER FIVE

Flirtation

I tore my attention away from this unique woman–waitress, bookkeeper, washer woman and now, mule skinner, to warm myself by the fire.

"General. General!"

Erastus was pointing down. I hurried over to see. Men were coming out of the warehouse, arms loaded with weapons. The long rifles were laid on the floodboards, then pistols and bullets filled the empty spots. There were five of the carts, three coaches, and loaded wagons with big wheels sank into the sand; enough guns and shot to arm fifty men or so. They would be sorely need by the time we reached Washington-on-the-Brazos where I anticipated at least that many volunteers waiting for me. I asked them all to bring their own rifle and shot and enough food for a month.

When the floorboards were back in place, the men distributed kegs of beer and boxes of liquor. The job was completed with slabs of salted bacon and sides of beef, wrapped in cheese cloth and jerky. Finally came tins of hardtack. With enough water and pepper—jalapeño was a favorite—you could eat it, hot or cold, spiced well.

When the last tin was in place, Emily finally looked up at our window, after a number of side-long glances. You bet I was still mad at her.

Then she smiled as if she knew I was reliving the near-scalding baptism. I tried to keep from smiling back, but I couldn't. With the morning sun playing shadows across her golden face, she looked animated, almost ethereal; although the wavy glass in the pane may have added to the ambiance of the moment.

She wore a simple checked dress, probably one made from several flour sacks. I know newspapers consider me flamboyant, and I will admit to a little passion for the colorful, but this morning I found a great comfort in the pedestrian. Her hair radiated black or deep brown, depending on where the sun hit it. The hint of chocolate complimented her complexion, somewhere between light brown and faded yellow. With the accompanying curves, she could be any man's sweet dream.

I nodded to acknowledge her silent greeting. She threw an embroidered valise into the back of the lead cart, then drew her dress to flash shapely leg as she climbed into the seat by the driver.

The caravan started off. After a few seconds, she turned and threw me a kiss.

Now what the hell did that mean?

CHAPTER SIX

Heading Out

The girls were chattering about steam trains as we rode along in our coach. The wagon captain had taken over the duties of getting the freight to Washington once we got underway, so I was relegated to riding with the other women in one of three Concord stagecoaches following the freight wagons. When we got Washington, I'd supervise the unloading and setting up the facilities for the convention. The rest of the women would serve the conventioneers in whatever capacity suited them. Suited the conventioneers, that is, not necessarily the women.

The subject of locomotives had come up because of how slowly we were going—perhaps half the speed of the normal stagecoach pace. We'd been ordered to stay with the freight wagons for protection. A humorous idea, as it turned out. We were not exactly with them, but behind them. If we opened the curtains, we'd freeze in the wet chill. If we closed them, we'd soon be suffocating in the humidity and our own odors—a combination of body aromas and perfumes intended to cover the same.

"Sort of like it is with trains," a girl named Colleen said. She sat across from me, a pert little thing with an upturned nose and scattered freckles on her alabaster skin. Blonde sausage curls framed her face. The only thing that marred her beauty was a missing front tooth, so she liked to keep her hand in front of her mouth when she talked.

"You leave the windows open, you get covered black as a nigger with soot and your clothes all burned full of holes with sparks from the engine, batting your skirts the whole way to keep from going up in flames."

No one paid any attention to how she'd insulted me, which was good in one way. It meant that I was accepted as part of the group even though I made no effort to pass for anything but the mulatto I am. On the other hand, I couldn't help think of my honey-colored mother and my chocolate-dark friends at home and wondered how many of these foul remarks I could take before I just blew up some day. But that day was not this day. Still and all I couldn't just let it pass.

I shifted in my seat to kind of settle my resentment, then said, "And you know how black those niggers can get." The conversation just went on, as if I were any other white person and not one of the "them" they'd been talking about. How magical is our blindness sometimes.

"At least that there locomotive's got some speed," big dark-haired Jill said. She sat beside me in the middle, her shoulders so broad she squeezed me and Kitty Jo up against the walls on each side. "You only have to put up with it for half the time."

"But the noise," Kitty Jo said. "There's not enough cotton in the world to plug your ears from all that rattling and squealing and creaking."

And so it went for a while. Eventually, silence fell except for some gentle snoring from those who the coach rocked to sleep. I peeked out the window, noted that we'd been out of sight of the gulf for some time now. At the moment I could see no water anywhere at all. Just sand and distant pines. It promised to be a tedious trip. I pulled a notebook and pencil from my carpet bag and added a few words to my ongoing letter to my mother.

It will be hard to credit, Mother, but it's the full truth that your housekeeper daughter made the acquaintance of a real general. His name is Sam Houston, and I believe you may be hearing a thing or two about him in the coming days.

Other than that, my life here continues much as before, and I count the days till I can leave Texas and wend my way back home. Now that Dr. Morgan has granted you manumission, we will not only be free, but will have enough money to open our inn. I hope your rheumatism is better. Be sure to keep smiling because it's that smile that sustains me through the long days and hard work.

Weariness is overcoming me now. I will write more later.

CHAPTER SEVEN

Jim Bowie

It was the knife stuck in his waistband. You didn't meet James Bowie without first noticing that knife sticking out of the blood red silk sash wrapped around his trim waist. No scabbard, the outline of the large blade bulging through the silk, anchored at the waist by the hand guard similar to drawing I've seen of 17th century swords. There are dozens of imitations, even a few made by his brother, Rezin, to cash in on the legend, but nothing as fascinating as the original, the one legend made famous. I chuckled at the thought.

Which legend? The one that claimed the original was forged from the steaming remains of a flaming star? The one about the duel which found him bound wrist to wrist with his adversary, the two men thrashing about in a dark saloon? The one that happened on some sandbar where Bowie defeated two men after being shot three or four times? No one seems to know how many there were, and I've never asked him the true number. Several men in the bar were stealing furtive glances at Bowie. I chuckled to myself, all they had to do to meet the legend was walk up, shake hands, and buy him a drink.

I had that knife in mind when I laid my proposition before him.

"Jim, I want you to go back to San Antonio and blow up the Indian mission."

His eyes widened, then narrowed as he cocked his head, fingering the handguard. "There are a number of missions there."

I had forgotten they were scattered all over the city, and I thought by calling it an Indian mission it would lessen the impact of my command.

"The one called the Alamo, the one downtown."

Bowie's height seemed to inflate above his six-three stature. Eyes narrowed, lips trembled, his hand caressed the thick hilt of his knife.

"Can't do it, General," he said, a hint of his Louisiana rearing up to cover the steel in his voice. "It's not some hovel or military prize. My wife's family has worshipped there for generations. Mission San Antonio de Valero is right around the corner from my home."

"You know General Cos is already on his way there. I suspect Santa Anna won't be far behind. We've got to destroy it. With its walls, the Long Barracks, and the chapel, it makes for a good base for operations, one we should deny the Mexicans."

"I don't know that I can," he said. "My father-in-law is alcalde. Hell, I'm the vice alcalde. You're asking me to destroy a house of worship in my own city."

Deef leaned in so he could hear over the din in the bar.

Bowie stood ramrod straight, his body as unbending as his rejection. I couldn't tell if this was religious fervor or Bowie's famous stubborn streak. You had to be a Catholic to be a Texican in this Mexican-dominated land. Both he and I had been baptized into the faith almost as soon as we crossed the Red River. It didn't mean you had to chant the rosary or tell the priest about a drunken Saturday night with one of Sarita's best girls. It was a rite of passage, a rite of citizenship. Of course, if you liked to take a nip or two, the religion offered convenient forgiveness by visiting a priest and dropping a coin or two in the poor box.

Still, his loyalty to family—especially that rapscallion brother—was as legendary as his blade.

Taking a deep breath, I reached for the rotgut, took a slow swig from the jug on the table. "Deef brought this back from a scouting trip to Refugio. It'll burn the hair off your throat and rot your gut, as advertised. Care for a swig before we go on?"

"I was wondering when you'd ask."

"Didn't need to till now." I handed him the jug, he laid it on his shoulder, tipped it his lips, and durn near emptied it.

"Leave any for me?"

"Not much." A sly grin stole over his face, deep-set grey eyes twinkling. I took a sip for myself and handed it back. He finished it off.

"You think you got me drunk enough to burn the city?" The liquor had fueled his voice so much it bounced off the walls.

Laughter filled the room; rough, boisterous. The men thought I'd been caught and this little drama could explode on me. They were waiting to see who won this little battle of wits.

"Not the whole city, just the best part for fortification. The Alamo. I hear Travis is there now. I could make it easy on you and dispatch orders to him."

"The hell you will."

"Just trying to be helpful."

"I take care of my own business. You've known me long enough to know that."

"Then take care of it."

"Damn right I will."

The whisky had not only raised the level of his voice, but loosened his tongue. I had gotten my promise, but I still wasn't sure Bowie would do it.

"Then you'd better get on back to San Antone and start planting dynamite. I'm off to powwow—one more time—with the Indians. Maybe they'll come in to help and we can give them a chunk of land. Our claims on Texas land run all the way to Canada. They could go up there and live free.

"After that, I'm going to the Constitutional Convention on Washington-on-the Brazos. We will become a great nation the day that document is signed but we have many dark and dangerous days ahead."

I stood and called to the room at large. "Are we ready?"

The question was met with a round of "huzzahs," "damn straight" and "let's get on with it."

"Then we'll meet at the convention and together we'll create the great Republic of Texas." More cheers.

"Barkeep, a round for the men here."

The men pushed toward the bar.

Bowie laughed and rushed to join them.

CHAPTER EIGHT

Attack

I thought at first it was thunder that awakened me that second night out. I'd consoled myself at sunset that we were perhaps halfway there and that the worst of the trip might be over. The wagon captain warned that the Brazos was a changeable stream and rising with the recent rains. He hadn't been over the road for some weeks, so we might run into difficulties with the way being flooded or washed out.

I just snuggled into my blankets, set my mind that all would go well, and concentrated on planning what we'd do when we arrived. We should have at least a week to set ourselves up, but you never know what the facilities are going to be like, so I was sure there'd be a lot to contend with. Clouds hid the moon, which was perfect for me to sleep as long as there were no cloudbursts, since it doesn't take much light to make me restless. I remember being deep into a dream, but the explosions wiped out all memory of it.

By the third blast, we all knew this wasn't just another storm and that the flashes in the night weren't lightning. The flat in the pines the captain had chosen for a camp had been too narrow to circle the wagons, so he'd put us double file, with us women sleeping under the coaches. A poor defense, as it turned out.

We must have been easy to spot, all clustered in our bedrolls. There were a couple of men on watch, but they probably went down in the first fusillade. All of us girls kept a firearm of some kind close by, things being what they are on the frontier, but everything happened so fast and there were so many of them, our guns weren't much use.

The greaser who came for me stumbled over Kitty Jo, fell down and lost his hat. I looked him in the eye and pulled the trigger of my pepperbox. His eye disappeared and he fell back. I thought afterwards about the fact that I'd probably killed a man and that there would be plenty of blood where that eye had been and maybe a hole in the back of his head. At the time, though, I was just glad to have him gone, and to tell the truth I haven't felt a twinge of regret since.

I saw Colleen point a derringer at her attacker, but he busted her in the mouth with the stock of his flintlock before she could use it. My first thought was that she'd just lost the rest of her front teeth. But she had worse troubles the second after when he started yanking her petticoats up over her head. And the second after that, someone wrenched my pepperbox from my hand and slammed me in the kidneys. Overwhelmed by pain and gasping for breath, I had no strength left to resist as they dragged me into the clearing and trussed me up—hands bound behind me—and dropped a slipknot around my neck.

It wasn't long before they had all of us in the same fix and were pulling us along behind their horses, two-by-two, headed for a place or a fate at which we could only guess. Sometimes I get strange thoughts in situations like this. Maybe it's a kind of protection against fear. This time, I started thinking how I'd describe all this in my letter to Mother.

Don't worry, Mama. Like you always said, as long as you're alive and fighting, you're winning. I'm not dead, and I haven't quit, so victory must be right around the corner.

CHAPTER NINE

Cherokee Chief

Chief Bowl snorted.

"You white men are like water easing around boulders in the river. You can feel it. You can even see it. But you can't catch it in your hand.

"You white men are like wind in the forest. You can see the leaves move. But you can't catch it in your hand.

"You—"

"Okay Chief, I got it." I didn't mind stopping him. It was his same old indictment of all things 'white man.' It didn't make this wily ol' Indian any difference that I held Cherokee citizenship.

"Here, Raven." He poked a well-worn peace pipe my way. I took it, the mouth piece well-worn wood on the end of a slim reed attached to a bowl made of clay harvested from a river bed and dried over a fire.

I took a little puff, just to be polite. Bowl's eyebrows raised, his eyes squinted. I didn't realize we were in the middle of a bona fide pipe ceremony, so I blew tobacco smoke to the four points of the compass.

"You have just sent breath as a bond to the Creator. Once a man does this, he cannot tell a lie."

"Nor can you Chief, whatever your decision."

We sat in silence—Chief Bowl, the tribe medicine man, Deef,

and myself.

"Look Chief, when I sit in your teepee I sit as a fellow Cherokee, the son of Chief Oolooteka, the powerful leader of the Cherokees in Arkansas territory, the husband of Tiana Rodgers, one of our own.

"Look." I held up my moccasin-clad foot. "I even wear moccasins made by your beloved granddaughter."

He nodded.

I paused. "I am the defender of the Cherokee in the land of the Great White Father. Witness how I dealt with the Indian agent who cheated your people last year."

That brought a grin to his face. "You nearly beat him to death."

"Not quite, but when I got through caning him, he wished he was dead. And the Cherokee were treated well."

Chief Bowl nodded his head, his thick braids bouncing. "I have a question for you, Raven. What would I expect to get out of this war between you and the half-breeds?"

To Chief Bowl the mixture of Aztec Indians and Spanish produced a unique heritage, one he considered half-breed because he hated the resulting breed known as Mexican and he had no love lost for the Aztecs who led the Spanish into his territory.

"They betrayed us. We agreed to not help the white man in their rebellion against Mexico and they promised us legal title to our land. They never kept their word. Now, a long time later you offer the same reward, under the same circumstances."

"You speak the truth, my brother."

Ten years before, a volatile American, Haden Edwards, had led a revolt against Mexico when he established what he called the State of Fredonia at Nacogdoches. At first Edwards had the support of the Indians, but when the Mexicans promised to give the Indians title to their land, they stepped aside. Edwards and his followers were driven back to the United States. Now I was asking Bowl to accept a similar promise from us.

"I give you my word as a Cherokee. Join us or at least don't take sides. I am on my way to Washington-on-Brazos where we will create on paper the Republic of Texas. Then we will drive the Mexicans out of our new nation. I will see to it that my colleagues agree that after our victory, you will receive title to your lands."

I held my hand out to Chief Bowl, whose eyes seemed to burn into me. "I give you my sacred pledge as a Cherokee, one brother to another. You will get your land."

He did not take my hand. "I will consider it."

He handed me that stinking, worn-out peace pipe. Once again, we addressed each of the cardinal compass points with a puff of smoke. Surrounding ourselves with our pledge. Bowl started to rise, but I raised a hand to stay him.

"One more matter, my friend. We sent an expedition from Morgan's Point. Wagons loaded with supplies for Washington-on-Brazos. There was food and drink and—I tell you this in confidence—considerable firearms. Santa Anna or someone ambushed the train, killed many men, and took everything."

"We have heard of this, Raven. It is a great loss for you, yes?"

"And perhaps a danger for you as well to have this army armed even better than before." He nodded.

"We will be aware."

"There were women. A dozen or more. No bodies were found, so we presume the Mexicans have taken them for their pleasure."

"It is often that way."

"There is one in particular, a mulatta. If you happen upon her. I would have her specially cared for."

"Let it be so."

As is the Indian way, he did not inquire about our relationship, which I appreciated, since I couldn't have explained it. My mouth was dry. I chewed my tongue to moisten it.

"Her name is Emily," I said. Why I added that unnecessary detail, I couldn't have explained, but I grew so uncomfortable I rose to my feet with a haste that bordered on rudeness. I forced myself to stop and obey the farewell rituals. Bowing, shaking hands, backing out of the tent.

How I was going to get the convention to honor my promise to Bowl I had no idea. But I had to turn my attention to victory over Santa Anna. Without that, it didn't matter what I promised to anyone.

CHAPTER TEN

Hostage

I tried to keep track of our route at first, but overland in the dark, I gave up in short order. As a result I had no idea of the location of the tent where I awoke. They'd thrown me in this hovel and left me alone. God knew where they'd taken the other women or what had happened to the teamsters. My hands were still bound, and I was dressed only in my drawers and camisole. They must have cut me out of my dress. Were the "they" men? Why hadn't I awakened? I'm not a sound sleeper. Something in the water they gave us, I supposed. We were all thirsting terribly after the ride. I didn't feel misused in my privates, though I feared that abuse awaited. I folded my arms across my breasts. That's when I realized my papers were gone.

I'd kept the contract with Dr. Morgan tucked into a pocket I'd sewn into my camisole as proof of my status as an indentured servant rather than a slave. Mexico had outlawed slavery—in law, if not entirely in fact—but on American soil without that paper, away from anyone who knew or could vouch for me, I was fair game for any slave trader looking to pick up ready cash for a healthy young female of my race. I couldn't have felt more naked had I been stripped and displayed in a public plaza. Whoever took it had complete power over me. I was sure I'd find out who that was soon enough. In the meantime, I required a chamber pot or I'd soon have to foul my quarters.

I crawled to the door of the tent, stuck my head out, and called for help. A light but steady rain was coming down. The soldier on guard, a kid of maybe 16, yelled, "*Dentro*," and waved the butt of his rifle in my face.

"*Baño*," I said. "*Necesito uno baño* right now."

I'd picked up some Spanish, but I still wasn't any good at it. He looked confused.

"*Yo urino por favor?*" I tried to think of a sign that wouldn't be obscene but failed. Somehow though I got across to him, and a look of panic crossed his face.

"*Sergento,*" he called. "*Venga. Es urgente.*"

And a sergeant did come running. "*Que paso?*"

They poured out a torrent of Spanish well beyond my understanding, but whatever they said resulted in my request being accommodated in short order. They refused my appeal to remove my bonds, and the bucket they provided was considerably less stylish than what I think of as a chamber pot, but it served its purpose. After I finished, I passed the stinking thing outside and took the opportunity to inventory my situation.

My small tent was one of a long row of others of the same size, and other rows stood before and behind us. I saw in the near distance a few larger tents. Officers no doubt. Everything looked white and clean. Soldiers in their white pants, blue tunics striped in red with white cross belts, stood post everywhere. With this many guards, escape would require great stealth. Or coquetry.

A woman—a girl, really, younger even than my guard—with broad-nosed, slant-eyed Indian features dressed in a sack of a muslin dress traded my chamber pot for a bucket of water with a rag floating in it. She gave me some directions of which I understood only the word "*limpia.*" Wash.

I smiled and said, "Gladly." She didn't smile, but tossed me a disdainful grunt and pointed her nose in the air as she walked off.

I completed my primitive toilet and slid the bucket out the tent door again, intending to find out what else I could about the camp. My little mistress was waiting. She grabbed the bucket and passed me a garment. A muslin dress much like her own, and gave me some more directions. I understood the words "*General*" and "*ahorita.*"

Another general. My second in a week. Won't Mother be really impressed now? Was it Santa Anna? Cos? Was I in the main camp of the Mexican army? The very people Houston came here to conquer? I'd have to speak to Dr. Morgan. This was a violation of my contract.

CHAPTER ELEVEN

Meeting Toño— March 01, 1836 51 days to San Jacinto

I could stand up in Santa Anna's tent, which felt wonderful after having crawled around on my hands and knees ever since I awoke. Two armed soldiers had marched me to the improvised headquarters and gestured me to enter. They remained outside in the wet. My hair was a curly friz—the more wet, the more it naps up—having resisted the puny comb that Isabella took to it. I longed for a ribbon to tidy it up, but none seemed available.

The general sat at a table covered with maps and pens. Soldiers flanked his chair. He rose when I entered, held out his hand to one of the soldiers, his eyes fixed on me the while. Once again I encountered a man whose height required me to tip my chin up to meet his eyes. I wondered if I'd ever see Houston again, wondered if he'd follow the instructions I'd left with the purse I'd secreted in his laundry.

The soldier placed a hat in the open hand, and the general donned a top piece that was of similar designed to his soldiers', but much taller and with a red plume in the front. Why, I don't know. Pure vanity, I supposed. Men. He was already tall enough without it. His coat was elegant—gold trim and braid around the buttons—and was heavy with medals and ribbons.

With a gesture, he directed me to sit in one of the two plush chairs in front of his table.

I said nothing, continued to stand, then took a step forward just to prove it wasn't because I'd failed to catch his meaning. I thought every small act of defiance I could manage might give me leverage for whatever waited.

He nodded to one of the men, who walked over and grabbed my shoulders, clearly intending to sit me down whether I wanted it or not. I threw off his hands, shot a fierce stare at Santa Anna and sat straight-backed on the front edge of the chair. He smiled. Pointed to my hands and said something to the man whom he'd sent to seat me. In a moment my hands were free, but my wrists and forearms where chafed raw. I rubbed them briefly, but refused to make a show of how much they hurt.

Santa Anna sat, removed his hat and passed it to his subordinate.

"Now, *Señorita*, it is time to tell me your name." His English was flawless, only slightly accented. I was told later it was only one of the foreign tongues he had mastered. At the time, I cared about none of that. I was just glad to have someone with whom I could communicate.

"First," I said, "I want to congratulate you on how well-ordered your camp is. It's a pleasure it is to be part of it. But if you wouldn't mind, I'd love to know where the other women are, why you kidnapped us, and what you intend."

"I am told you shot one of my men. Shot and killed him."

"He seemed anxious to die. I obliged him."

"We have a right to protect our sovereign nation from invaders."

"Since when did transporting supplies become an invasion?"

Santa Anna smiled again. Or rather smirked. "Supplies. Yes."

So he'd found the guns. No surprise there.

"My name, *Señorita*, is General Antonio López de Santa Anna. I have other names, but as a gringa, a gringa mulata, you would neither recall nor understand them if I told you. Your people neither recall nor understand anything about our people. One title you might comprehend is The Napoleon of the West. Do you know why they call me that?"

I knew exactly, naturally. Everyone in these parts did, but I wanted to hear what he'd say. "I thought Napoleon was French," I said.

The smile disappeared, and he leaned toward me, fisted his hands on the table. Fire shot from his eyes as from cannons. I admit the force of it took me aback.

"I led our armies against the oppressor Spaniards, an enemy no one thought we could defeat, yet we threw them out of our country and became an independent nation. And now your Houston and your Austin and your other power-hungry countrymen want to take it away from us. They believe we are weaklings. Mestizo insects they can squash. The Spaniards believed the same thing. The past is prologue to the future. Have you heard that?"

I had, somewhere, but I wanted no link between us. "Nope," I said.

I stayed on the edge of my seat. Tried to remain nonchalant, but this was one impressive man with a mission and the conviction to back it up. I began to fear a little for my other general.

"So." He sat down, smiled again. "Perhaps we can begin once more. Your name, please?"

"You may call me Miss West," I said. He continued smiling, waiting. His eyes fired again. I hadn't intended to say it, but after a moment I went ahead with it. "Emily West."

He leaned back, and what came next was almost a whisper.

"Good. Then Emily is what I will call you. And when you return for our evening meal, you will please to call me the same name my beloved wife does. Can you guess what it is, *gringa mulata* Emily?"

I shook my head.

"'Toño.' It comes from 'Anthony.' Please not to forget it. Toño and Emily. A nice sound is it not?"

I nodded, which wasn't enough of an answer for him. The eyes fired up again.

"Is it not?" The volume stayed the same, but the intensity fairly doubled.

"Yes," I said.

He lifted his eyebrows.

"Yes, sir, Toño, sir." I saluted. I don't think he liked either the "sir" or the salute, but it seemed I'd satisfied him enough for the moment.

"Good. And now you will leave me to my work, and you will go to prepare yourself. Isabella will help you. *Hasta luego*, Emily."

"*Hasta luego*," I said, but I was speaking to the top of his head. He was staring down at his maps as if I'd suddenly vanished. "Are you sure that map's not upside down?"

He actually started to check the map. Stopped himself. Realizing I'd succeeded in tricking him. He looked up at me. His mustache twitched, but I couldn't tell whether he was amused or angry.

"Well," I said, "it wouldn't do to find ourselves going north when we wanted to go south, now would it?" The sound of a new downpour sounded like rapid gunfire on the tent roof. He started to smile, caught himself, and shooed me away.

I don't know what I'd expected when they brought me to Santa Anna, but nothing had gone the way I might have predicted. And I was sure this evening's meal would be more of the same.

CHAPTER TWELVE

Dining With The General

The rain had stopped by the time I made my command appearance at the general's table. He'd supplied me with a brocade gown that was only a little too small—My ankles showed; my shoulders and bodice felt constrained—and I looked quite elegant for a military camp. The general himself looked elegant enough for a state dinner, and the table shone in the lantern light with silver, porcelain, and crystal. A private held my chair, and Santa Anna waited till I was seated at the foot of the table before he took his place at the head. My attendant, Isabella, entered bearing a decanter of *vino tinto*, filled both our glasses, then retired to the sideboard where she stood, doubtless awaiting further instructions. I'd have felt more at home in her place.

"And to the lovely Emily," Santa Anna said, lifting his glass, "may our union be a long and pleasant one."

I smiled, but kept my hands in my lap. His manners were more gracious than the plain approach of General Houston, but behind his tone and smirk I sensed an uncompromising brutishness.

He smiled, put his glass back on the table, and rose. He smiled all the way to my chair, smiled all the while he raised my glass, smiled all the while he gripped my wrist and wrenched and raised my arm. The lacerations from the rope were still painful, and the vice of his fist exacerbated those as well as adding, I was sure, bruises. He brought his cheek next to mine and growled in my ear.

"It is polite, Emily, to respond when the host proposes a toast, yes?" I grimaced, said nothing. "Now, if you will take the glass, *por favor.*"

I did as he asked, and he released his grip. He returned to his seat. He raised his glass again.

"Now. May we drink to our union?"

I kept my glass raised, but did not drink. "Before I do, General—"

"Toño," he interrupted.

"Toño," I said. "Perhaps you can clarify the details of this so called union you have in mind."

"Those, Miss Emily, will be a matter of mutual agreement as matters proceed." He put his glass to his lips and drank. I did not follow. He fired those eyes again, and I decided that perhaps this was not the time to fight, so I wet my lips with the wine, which I recognized as a fine vintage."

"*Bueno, Señorita.* Now, Isabella, the first course, if you please."

Isabella exited and returned with a silver soup tureen. She placed it carefully in the center of the table, glanced at Santa Anna, who nodded, then lifted the lid. I gasped. After I saw what it contained, though, I realized I should have expected it.

"I see you recognize the contents, Emily."

I nodded, could not speak. The tureen held not food, but my missing contract. Santa Anna nodded to Isabella, who lifted the parchment, holding it between two fingers while the general continued.

"When I read it, I realized how fortunate it was that we discovered you. Fortunate, that is, for you." He nodded again. Isabella picked up a candle.

"You were a mere servant. In America, without this flimsy document, you might be mistaken for a slave, yes?"

It was my turn to nod, but I was speechless, seeing what was about to transpire.

"However, under my protection, you have no need for this." Isabella applied flame to my contract. "You are free of all such obligations and threats of bondage."

The contract leapt into flames, and Isabella dropped it into the tureen.

My cheeks—my entire face—burned hot as a skillet. I felt as if my soul itself was ablaze. I clutched my skirt and bit my tongue so hard I tasted blood. I imagined Joan of Arc watching English torches ignite the kindling at her feet, knowing the blaze would soon consume her entirely.

The red and yellow flames lasted only a moment, but they will dazzle my memory forever. They soon transformed into black flakes. At that, the fire in me turned to a cold emptiness, as if a great cavern had opened within me. I felt drained of all strength. Only my determination to show no weakness before this arrogant tyrant with his leering smile kept me from sinking to the floor in sobs.

The necessity to conceal my distress remained, but I realized the stubborn resistance I'd been exhibiting to this point would not succeed. It was time for a change in tactics. I picked up my wine glass, gaining some courage to see that the liquid did not tremble as I raised it.

"It is plain I owe you much, general—"

"Toño," he corrected me.

"Toño. This new…alliance between us holds great promise. I propose a toast to burned bridges and new beginnings."

We looked at one another over our glasses as we drank. If my sudden acquiescence had aroused suspicion, he didn't show it. His shoulders squared and his eyes twinkled like stars. Stroking a man's ego is as dependable a ploy as stroking his privates if you want to bring him to attention.

"Beauty and eloquence as well, I see. You are a prize, indeed, Emily. Isabella, the next course, if you please."

Isabella exited, and I gently turned the conversation in another direction.

"Toño, I want you to know how much I appreciate your hospitality."

"*Por nada,*" he said.

"However, I'm puzzled. Why me? There were twelve of us women in the coaches. Any one of them could be seated where I am."

"True, Emily, true," he said.

Isabella returned carrying a platter containing a roast duck surrounded by thinly-sliced potatoes. She presented the dish to the general, who nodded his head in approval, then she carried it to the sideboard and began carving.

Isabella laid our plates before us. I smiled and thanked her. Santa Anna raised his fork as a signal that it was time to begin eating. I was starving and fell to immediately. Santa Anna picked up the thread.

"You understand, Emily, none of the other women had your skill and courage. Nor, I might add, your complexion, shaded like the earth. Not like the Americanos, pale as skulls, most of them."

He stroked my cheek. I managed not to pull away.

"You, Mullata, are like a yellow rose. Delicate in color, petals soft to the touch, but you do have thorns I'll have to watch."

"How gracious of you, to compare me to a such a blossom," I said, smiling. I left the thorns unmentioned, but hoped they would make effective weapons before this was finished.

"And where are the others?" I asked, trying to make it sound like polite conversation.

"They are in various other quarters, engaged in activities similar to yours, though in less sumptuous surroundings. Not that an army encampment can do justice to what you deserve."

So he'd distributed the girls to his officers like so many appetizers. I'd been honored as the main course.

The duck finished, Santa Anna, ordered our wine glasses refilled and sent Isabella for what turned out to be a joint of venison on a bed of bay leaves. Gorgeous as it looked, this was going to be more than I could stomach, but I knew I must pretend.

"Now, my dear young lady, I have a question. Where were you bound with these supplies?"

This surprised me. Did he really not know about the upcoming convention at Washington-on-the-Brazos?

"I'm not sure," I said. "My boss at Morgan's point told us to get in the coaches and follow the wagon train. We were headed north and told it would take about a week to get wherever we were going and that we'd get more instructions when we arrived. Beyond that . . . " I shoved a piece of venison into my mouth.

"And the firearms?"

I raised my eyebrows and coughed my meat on to the plate, half-chewed. After a swallow of wine, I fanned my face with a napkin, feigning recovery as much as I'd feigned the attack. "Forgive my manners, please, Gen—Toño—but you shock me. What would we be doing with guns? All I saw were barrels and casks of beer and whisky, and such as that."

He stared at me for some moments. There was no fire, just a searching look, probably trying to decide whether I was lying. I leaned forward, smiled, raised my glass as a signal to Isabella for more. He apparently took my request, as I'd intended, as a sign that I wanted to get on with our feast. Finally he smiled, lifted his own glass. We drank, and I leaned back in my chair, relaxed a bit. He mirrored my movements.

"What did you do with my dress?" I was feeling a bit woozy.

"It was dirty, bloody. Unfit for such as you."

"Such as me?"

"One capable of taking charge of supervising the loading of wagons, taking care of valuable *merchandise.* And of proposing beautiful toasts. You see, Miss Emily, we know quite a lot about you."

But he didn't, apparently, know about the convention in Washington. What did he know, not know, pretend to know or not to know? This conversation was going to take more navigation than I felt capable of in my present state. But I had no choice.

"Where is Señor Houston's army, Miss Emily?" He looked at my glass. "Please, I would not like you to lack for food or drink."

"I don't think—" I started to object but he interrupted.

"Please."

I smiled, sipped. He looked again. I sipped again. More this time. Isabella refilled my glass.

"Now." He continued.

"I know nothing about an army. I knew nothing about guns. I did withhold from you that we were headed for Washington-on-the-Brazos. There is a convention there soon. What is this army you're talking about?"

"Convention?"

"It's some kind of politics. Look, Toño. You saw the contract. I'm a servant for Dr. Morgan. I work in his warehouse and his hotel. That's all I do and who I am. I came to Texas for one year to earn some money, then return home."

"But now, your life has taken a different direction, no? You do not care for the venison?"

I looked down, almost surprised to find food in front of me. "I'm sorry. It has been a difficult time. My appetite seems to have vanished."

"Understandable, certainly. Perhaps dulces will help." He nodded to Isabella, who took away my plate, the venison, and—thank the Lord—my wine glass.

Now Santa Anna and I were alone except for the ubiquitous private in the corner, who seemed no more than furniture.

"Toño," I said. "May I ask you a question?"

"Ah, but Emily you did just ask me a question." I managed a smile. "You see, I am not all business. I have a sense of humor, yes?"

"Yes," I said, "Yes you do. But may I ask another?"

He pointed, laughed. I chuckled myself. "All right, you have me a second time. However, I was wondering about the men. The ones on the wagon train. What happened to them?"

"Ah, your drivers and the rest. Perhaps you had a sweetheart among them?"

"Since you seem to know so much about me, you probably already know," I said, "that is not the case." He smiled and nodded, glad to accept credit for knowing all. "However, I had friends among them. I would care to know of their fate."

"Your friends, Miss Emily, the ones who survived our first attack, scattered like rabbits before our soldiers. Which they will no doubt do should they be foolish enough to challenge my army in the future."

"How many did you kill?" Before he could answer, if, indeed, he intended to answer, Isabella returned with the sweet cakes.

"And these, my dear Miss Emily, will settle your stomach. Along with a touch of Brandy, of course."

My stomach turned at the thought, but given the way previous encounters had gone, I submitted to a few nibbles and sips while the General held forth on the prowess of his military force. The wine must have had a bit of an effect on him as well or he wouldn't have boasted to someone like me that he was headed for a showdown at San Antonio with well over a thousand trained and disciplined troops while all Houston would be able to muster was a laughable force of half that many poorly-armed vagabonds. Maybe he thought it would put me in a romantic mood to find myself in the company of someone so powerful. All it made me feel was relieved that he appeared to have abandoned further interrogation for the time being. He returned to the subject of the convention.

"I hope I did not appear to need military intelligence from you, Miss Emily, about this business on the Brazos. My questions sought confirmation only. This gathering at Washington is an entertainment for politicians, as you have already surmised. It would be a waste of time to attack it, though our men do appreciate the spirits you've provided, and we can always use more firepower.

"I know that the Americanos are assembling a considerable force at San Antonio and that these guns were ultimately bound for there. No matter. They will flee to the bushes once again like *los Conejos*, and we will be done with their foolishness for good."

He rose, dabbed at his lips with his napkin. "In the meantime…" he executed a sweeping gesture with his arm, then nodded to the private, who drew back the tent wall. Except it proved not to be a wall at all, but a curtain. When he pulled it back, it revealed couch and blankets and pillows.

I'd known something like this awaited me the while, of course. I was not a stranger to the arts of the boudoir, nor neither was I an habitué. I'd lain with only two men, and with neither for money nor against my will. However, it was out of the question to refuse the general, and I knew I must appear to be not only willing, but delighted. Still, I determined to give of myself only what was required and nothing more. My mother often talked of her slavery in terms of scripture, of giving unto Caesar, and that's how she kept her dignity even in the most undignified of circumstances. "This way, my dear Emily," he said. He was unbuttoning his tunic as he spoke.

"Yes sir," I said. He gave me that fiery look again.

"*Sí,* Toño," I said. I stepped toward the chamber. By this time, his outer garment hung loosely. He grasped my elbow as I passed. I winced at the pressure.

"Such a dusky, lovely beauty," he whispered, squeezing even tighter.

This promised to be no gentle evening.

CHAPTER THIRTEEN

Paseo

The sun came out the next morning, and they paraded us around the camp mud like trophies, Santa Anna and his officers did. Laughing and nuzzling, demanding we cuddle up to them, advertising to the world and no doubt pretending to themselves that they'd performed seductions instead of rapes.

I counted women as I strolled. Someone was missing. "Toño," I said. I refused to call him *"Mi Amor,"* as he demanded, and he'd acquiesced, thinking probably that he'd persuade me eventually. It always serves well to withhold something, even a crumb. "What happened to Colleen?" I said.

"¿Como?"

"The girl with blonde hair and very white skin."

"Ah, the one without teeth. None of my officers found her attractive enough for dalliance, so she has duties in the kitchen."

A scullery maid, doubtless despised and abused by the other women. And I wagered to myself that she'd be placed in the charge of some soldier of lesser rank. I shuddered, pitied her, even beyond the rest of us.

Hoofbeats sounded. A soldier on horseback reined his palomino to a stop in front of Santa Anna, splattering us with mud left behind by the recent rain.

52

"General," he yelled. He leaped to the ground, clicked his heels, saluted, and shoved a dispatch into Santa Anna's hands.

The general scanned it briefly, then began calling names. "Mendez, Tejada, Mejias. *Vengan ahorita.*"

Three officers abandoned their ladies and hurried to salute and stand at attention before him. He issued orders, sending them scurrying off, shouting orders of their own. The ladies who had been on their arms stood bewildered, as the camp suddenly became a turmoil of activity.

Santa Anna did not abandon me quite so suddenly as the others had their women. "*Disculpe, Senorita.* We have received word that your people have begun their operations in San Antonio sooner than expected. We must hurry forth to give them the greeting they deserve."

"Toño, what will happen to me now that you are leaving?"

"My dear Emily, surely you don't think I would leave you behind."

"How far is San Antonio?"

"I promise you will be well taken care of, *mi amor*, every step of the way. And your sisters as well, since I know you worry about them. Wait here for a few moments. I have already directed that Isabella come to assist you all in preparing for the journey. Now, if you'll excuse me." And he trotted off.

The air filled with dust fair to dim the sun and shouts and yells ricocheted everywhere. Men folded tents and hitched wagons. I saw mules being hitched to the very coaches that had brought us from Morgan's point.

Santa Anna's words of assurance gave me no comfort. I needed information to plan an escape. The current confusion might create an opportunity, but I couldn't just dash off without some idea of which direction to go.

I knew almost nothing of Texas outside the area around Morgan's Point. San Antonio was somewhere vaguely to the west, but how far or how to get there I had no idea. If I could escape near the Brazos and follow the river to Washington … But I didn't even know whether to go east, west, north, or south. It was encouraging that Santa Anna was headed for wherever Houston was, but I had no wish to be behind Mexican lines when and if it came to a battle.

So I'd be forced to wait and scheme and listen. I swallowed down a sob and forced my shoulders back at the thought being forced to endure more nights like the previous one, which had left me sore in the nether regions and bruised in a number of other parts as well. The general was not so much a lover as a marauder. Words that on the lips of other men might constitute terms of endearment were from him commands of attack. And he had the stamina of a warrior to go with his violent impulses. Pain and humiliation, I feared, were to be my constant companions until I could find a way out. That way out had to come soon, for I didn't know how long I could preserve that core of myself that saved me from despondency, on other far side of which lay despair and resignation. I felt my body sagging again, forced my shoulders back once more.

Isabella arrived in a great frenzy.

"*Senoritas,*" she said. And began a flurry of gestures and commands from which I recognized the word *prisa.* But I needed no words to understand that she wanted us to hurry, hurry, hurry. Back to my tent. Off with my dress-up, gown, back into the plain muslin dress I'd worn for my introduction to Santa Anna.

When I emerged from my tent, Isabella was right there to rush me and the other girls like a herd dog driving a flock of geese to our coaches, whence we were ushered in and seated. The door closed, and an armed soldier stood outside.

Santa Anna had promised we'd be well taken care of. It looked like that meant well-guarded. I was again seated beside broad-shouldered Jill, with Kitty Jo squeezed against the opposite side of the coach. The sight of Colleen across from me nearly brought me to tears. She was smeared with grease and soot from head to toe. Her hair hung lank and filthy—given her penchant for curls, a true bit of humiliation. I wished I could have passed her a few of mine. Her hands lay clasped in her lap, her eyes cast down to the floor.

I leaned forward and touched her hand, intending a bit of tender comfort. She squealed and jumped back, eyes startled, and her nearly toothless mouth gaped in fear. Then she saw it was me, tried a smile, then resumed her previous attitude. That over, we looked at each other, all searching for words. Jill finally broke the silence.

"Well," she said to no one in particular, "how was yours?"

CHAPTER FOURTEEN

Brazos and Flight

It didn't take us long to find the Brazos, as it turned out. On the second day, heading straight into the setting sun, we set up camp on its banks. We were to cross it the following day, though, swollen as it was by the downpour from the storm that had passed through, it didn't look like a promising ford to me, both banks swampy and the water too murky to judge its depth. But, once again, I wasn't in charge.

They delivered us beans in tin cups for dinner along with a beverage they called coffee but which I suspect was heated swamp water. A comedown from the venison and duck and wine Santa Anna had served me, but it came at a much lower price. We'd waited hours—having no clock, I can't say how long—in our coach waiting to leave. They brought a canteen in response to our request for water and a kitchen pot for our other needs. My bruises ached, and my spirits sank to think that my letter to Mother was lost and the chance to start a new one uncertain at best.

After Jill broke the ice, we all traded stories of our liaisons. Some of us were luckier than others, having drawn men who overindulged themselves in the captured liquor, rendering them sleepy and ultimately unable to perform. Others were forced to submit not only to their assigned partners, but to friends invited to the festivities. I determined that my fortunes fell somewhere in the midpoint of our collective misery. Colleen pulled her hair across her face like a screen and would say not a word.

So here we sat beside the Brazos I hoped that the press of business would keep Santa Anna from calling for me this night as it had last night. I had said nothing of my idea that traveling upriver would bring us to safety. I felt bad about leaving my sisters behind, but I didn't see how I could possibly get all twelve of us a distance of perhaps a hundred miles with soldiers in pursuit. A painful decision, but anything I did I had to do on my own.

Of course, Santa Anna's troops might be too busy getting to San Antonio to chase us, but I didn't think my general's pride would allow me to flee without pursuit. Besides, having been in his camp, we had military information he might consider valuable, though aside from the troop numbers Santa Anna let slip, I didn't think we'd seen anything significant. He would certainly know about the expedition to San Antonio. But my dear Toño might not see things that way.

As I finished my beans and strolled around the campfire, assessing my opportunities, it seemed my supposed plan was but fantasy. Three pickets stood near our coaches, in addition to the other pickets who surely surrounded the perimeter of the whole camp. Supposing I did get beyond them, what was I to do?

My clothes were not suited to walking, and I knew not where to get better. From my girlhood days in Dr. Morgan's house on the Hudson, I knew something about foraging around a river, knew how to catch a frog, even how to snare a crane or heron, so perhaps I could provision myself enough to survive for a while.

I heard horses snuffling and stamping, so knew a remuda was nearby. Perhaps I could use one of them to get away. Hoping to appear meandering without purpose, I let my steps gradually carry me beyond the light of the fire into the darkness and toward the horses. It wasn't long before I saw the herd, perhaps two dozen hobbled and within a rope corral. Pickets stood every few yards around them. Santa Anna may not have feared Texicans, but he did fear Indians, who had been trained since they could walk in the art of horse-stealing. As for me, I feared them all.

I hugged myself, trying to still the quaking inside me. Toño was a cruel man, but he kept me warm and fed, and he did not beat or whip me as some of the other soldiers did to my Morgan's Point companions. I imagined the pain of a rifle ball in my back as I tried to flee, the thirst and starvation that could await me alone on the plains. Or Indians. According to tales I'd heard, Toño was a saint compared to them— especially the Apaches. I'd never let fear stop me from taking a chance before, but I'd never faced danger like this.

How I was to get near enough to steal a horse, I couldn't imagine. It certainly wouldn't be tonight. Perhaps during the crossing tomorrow. I eased my way back toward the fire, felt a presence behind me, turned, and found myself staring into the general's eyes. My hopes to avoid his attentions this evening were dashed. I tried not to let my disappointment show. The Brazos River was said to be named for the arms of God, but God didn't seem to be anywhere around, and Santa Anna's arms were another story entirely. Yet, it meant everything for the moment to stay in his good graces, so I managed to recover quickly.

"Toño," I said, my hand fluttering at my breast. "You startled me. What a surprise. A pleasant surprise. I thought … I was afraid you'd forgotten me."

"My apologies for neglecting you last night, *querida*. Press of duties. But tonight, I am yours. *"Por Aqui."*

And he led the way toward his quarters, which were behind temporary canvas curtains, with no roof. And that night, my eyes to the stars, Santa Anna's groaning in my ear, his loins thrusting at mine, I whispered the words he'd been begging to hear.

"Toño, *mi amor verdadero*, My true love."

He raised his head and looked into my eyes, smiling, little knowing that what I'd just uttered was the first part of my plan to flee him and his army forever.

CHAPTER FIFTEEN

Crossing Over

The fording of the Brazos was not complete until well into the following night's darkness. With the river so high, progress was slow and difficult. Toño became enraged when a wagon equipped with log pontoons capsized and dumped an artillery piece into the water. Attempts recover the gun from the murky water failed.

I hadn't eaten all day, but the cries of the unfortunate men who had been in charge of the cannon, the crack of the whips that ripped the skin from their backs, left me with no appetite to touch the few spoonsful beans and rice that were supposed to constitute our supper.

We women looked at one another in silence, stiffened at each scream of pain. Some of them recalled their own beatings only days earlier. After the flogging finally stopped, I managed to cram down a few bites of my supper. I couldn't afford to skip meals if I was to succeed in escaping. And if I had ever seriously considered staying in camp for the comforts of Toño's tent, those cries had purged the idea.

Afterward, the women drifted off into the darkness. Somehow, our togetherness had been important during the punishments, but now it seemed a time for solitude. Except for Colleen, who wore a sad smile as she approached me. She no longer bothered to cover her toothless gums, and her hair hung tangled and unbrushed almost to the middle of her back. Either they'd beaten the pride out of her or she'd figured that it had been worth trying to hide one missing tooth, but hopeless to hide the nakedness that remained now.

I reached out and drew her down to sit beside me. "Hello, Colleen. I guess we're lucky we didn't drown today."

She nodded, glanced at me, then looked at the ground. She spoke in a voice so low I could barely hear it.

"Emily, will you see the general tonight?"

"I never know. I hope not this late. I hope always never to see him again."

"You're his favorite, Emily. We all know that. Couldn't you ask him … " Her voice trailed off..

"Ask him what, Colleen?" I leaned toward her, afraid I'd miss her answer if she gave one. As it turned out, there was no danger of that. She turned and almost yelled in my face.

"Ask him to give me to one of them. Only one. Not pass me around like a toy. You can't know how horrible it is, with my mouth the way it is they all … " she collapsed into a puddle of sobs and tears.

I'd been lamenting my own situation, but compared to Colleen I was a queen, and my throat swelled shut when I tried to speak. Her misery, my guilt at being so much better off, my pain at being in my awful situation tore through me like wildfire. I reached out, pulled back, finally got to my knees and laid my hands on her shoulders.

"Of course I will, Colleen," I said. "It's the least I can do." And it occurred to me that perhaps I could do more than that, for both of us.

CHAPTER SIXTEEN

Flight. Almost.

Several days out from the Brazos, Colleen and I had worked out a plan. Santa Anna had granted her request. He'd ordered that the sergeants and corporals draw lots to determine whose paramour she'd become. Corporal Santiago, a youngster of no more than sixteen, won the lottery. For Colleen, he was ideal. Callow and shy, the youth made few attempts to force her, and she found him easy to thwart when he did. She'd regained some of her pride, even gathered her hair into a bun and washed her face.

I was optimistic, almost giddy at the notion of escaping, and I knew that with Colleen as a partner I stood a much better chance than I would alone. Colleen's sojourn with her many lovers—rapists—had one advantage. Where I had been isolated with Santa Anna, carefully watched both by Isabella and the soldiers, she had seen a great deal of the camp, had been able to observe the soldiers' routines. She knew who was conscientious, who was lax, and which hours they kept watch. It was almost thrilling to watch her spirits revive at her new situation and at the opportunity to help us get away.

"You are my life, Emily," she said. I held up my palm and shook my head. "Yes you are, and I won't hear different. And I've discovered just what we're looking for. There's a filthy no-good sergeant named

Molina who snoozes his way through his picket duty. He guards the horses. I bet we could steal one and slip right by him."

"And be on our way back east to Washington-on-the-Brazos. I feel certain we can depend on General Houston's protection," I said. I told Colleen nothing of my other thoughts of what might pass between Houston and myself. I barely told myself of such thoughts.

"Colleen," I said, "I knew I'd picked the right partner. I have just that more ploy to execute, then we'll be on our way."

She fairly leaped to embrace me. "Oh, Emily, you are my life."

"You said that," I replied.

"I can't say it enough times." She was weeping now.

"Remember. If we're caught … And even if we're not, we'll be alone. There are many dangers out there, and with the weather so chancy … "

"Worse than this, Emily?" She shook her head. "Not possible."

"Then we have only one more ploy to accomplish, and we'll be ready," I said, which triggered another embrace and more tears.

"Calm yourself, Colleen. You mustn't give us away."

And, indeed, she straightened up, dried her tears, and walked away as if we had just been talking about the weather. My confidence soared.

***

"Toño, *mio*," I said as he lay by my side that night, nearly in slumber after his lovemaking. It was our first night together in three days because he'd been consumed with keeping the army moving toward San Antonio. Ordinarily, I'd have welcomed the respite, but now his absence threatened to undo my strategy and I'd become fretful, snapping at Isabella and whoever else crossed my path. I caught myself brushing my hands across my skirts as if to shoo away flies of anxiety. Finally, though, he was here, and I felt this was the time.

"*Sí, querida?* he mumbled sleepily.

"Toño, I am tired of riding in that bumpy coach jammed cheek to jowl with the other women."

"Only a few more days, *querida*," he said.

"Those days seem to last a lifetime. I was hoping … but never mind."

"Finish what you started, Emily."

"It's unreasonable. I shouldn't have bothered you."

"Emily." It was his teasing, warning tone. He was awake, up on one elbow. Just what I wanted, but I still almost lost my courage. He was anything but gullible. If he should guess … But I forged ahead.

"Perhaps you could let me ride horseback. It could be only part of the day, not all day. What could it hurt? Isabella could ride with me. It would be such a welcome change."

"We have no sidesaddles," he said.

"Toño," I placed a fingertip on the tip of his nose and gave him an impish grin. "Have you ever ridden sidesaddle?"

He grasped my hand and kissed it. "Don't be ridiculous."

"Then don't you be ridiculous. Sidesaddle, indeed."

"But, Emily, in the coach you are safe." His eyes narrowed. He was suspicious. My stomach fisted up. In a honeyed voice, he continued. "On a horse, there are prairie dog holes, Indian arrows. Not to mention the weather—sun, rain, wind—on your delicate skin." And I knew I had him. General though he was, he was still a man, and subject to all the vanities of his sex.

"My delicate skin. Oh, Toño," I gushed, "you are so wonderful and considerate. I'll wear a straw hat to prevent burning and with the fresh air, I'll look even more beautiful for you. And Toño, I saw the most precious little sorrel mare in the remuda yesterday. She would be perfect. Oh, please, please, please." I embellished my plea with multiple kisses to his lips and cheeks, cradling his head between my hands.

"*Querida, querida,*" he said, "let me breathe, please." He pushed me gently away, smiling. "You shall have your sorrel. I will find a mount for Isabella. For your protection from the elements, you will ride in the morning hours only. After midday, you will return to the coach."

I was not deceived by Santa Anna's statement about "protection from the elements." During the morning hours, he could count on his minions to remain vigilant. After noon, although there was no siesta on such a march as this, their customary habit of a midday slumber made them less alert to any inclination I might have to flee. Nevertheless, I threw myself at him in a manner reminiscent of how Colleen had embraced me earlier. I tried to appear as vulnerable and emotionally delicate as she. "You are not a general, Toño, you are a prince. A king."

"And a man with many duties." He pushed me away again, not so gently this time, and began dressing. "I may not see you again for a few days, I regret to say."

I manufactured a pout. "Oh, Toño—"

He held up a hand. "No tears now, Emily. You must remain strong. We have been marching hard, yet we must increase our pace. We have received word that Houston has left Washington-on-the-Brazos and is headed to San Antonio. I expect a grand battle there. Our victory will be glorious and final."

My heart froze. Even if we escaped, General Houston—my real general—was on the move. How were Colleen and I to find him?

"*Hasta Luego, querida,*" Santa Anna said. His farewell embrace was perfunctory, his mind already on other matters. And so was mine. How quickly things change. How quickly we must adapt or perish.

CHAPTER SEVENTEEN

On Our Way

We gave it three more days. Time enough, we hoped, for my little horse, whom I'd christened Anna, supposedly in honor of the general, but really just because I needed a name to call her as I got her sufficiently accustomed to me not to raise a fuss when I approached her during the night. I was not sentimental about what that name was, and "Anna" served its purpose.

As the hour grew near, the thought of wandering alone over the open plains, unsure of Houston's location or how to find him was so frightening it almost stopped us. We felt how cold one another's hands became as we talked about running out of food and water, about bandits, Indians, accidents. A mere ankle sprain could finish us.

We considered staying with Santa Anna until San Antonio, then sneaking through the battle lines. But our current plight was even more intolerable than our fear of the unknown. Colleen's boy, not a threat in himself, had begun renting her out, so that her situation was really no better than it had been before she'd been assigned to him. We finally determined to try intercepting Houston's army on its way from east to west from Washington to San Antonio. If we failed, we would continue north to the United States. How we were to accomplish all that with one horse and whatever few provisions we'd be able to purloin we didn't know. It helped to look on the whole thing as a glorious adventure rather than a journey through the underworld. Like making a novel out of the romance of our lives. Honey can sweeten the bitterest tea.

So, at the dark of the moon as we approached the Colorado River with the camp swarming with the confusion of preparing for the next day's crossing, we slipped up on Sergeant Molina, who was using his musket as a prop to keep him from falling to the ground in his customary half-slumber.

"*Sargento*," I whispered, tracing a finger across his whiskered cheek. He mumbled as if in a dream, then lifted his lids a bit, then opened his eyes wide in amazement to see who had spoken.

"*¿Señorita, que paso?*" he said. At which point, Colleen smacked the back of his head with a rock.

He dropped in a heap, and we moved fast, scarcely breathing for fear of discovery. I went for Anna, whom I retrieved with little difficulty. I tried for a second mount, but excited too much snuffling and pawing. When I returned to Colleen, she'd gathered what she could from Molina's person—his musket, ammunition pouch, belt, the cross-straps from his uniform—everything we thought we could carry to help us through the journey to come. With the lead from Anna's hackamore in one hand along with the small bag of corn bread and stew meat and portions of Molina's uniform bundled in the other, I set off in the dark. Colleen followed with the musket and other necessaries. The remuda was at the edge of the camp, and the usual outer posting of guards was engaged in other activities connected with the imminent fording of the Colorado, so we had no more to worry about. Until they discovered we were gone. Which would be soon.

We moved as quickly as we could, not very fast, as disorganized and laden down we were. With the campfires still in sight, but a good distance away, we dropped down into a gully and set about consolidating ourselves.

First, there was the matter of clothing. There was no question of travelling in our long skirts, and we had no trousers. Colleen was better off than I because she was wearing a skirt and blouse. At Santa Anna's insistence, I spent each day in a full dress, complete with corset. Thus, I had to remove my complete outer layer to render myself mobile, which left me in corset, camisole, and drawers. Colleen at least had a blouse to cover her camisole. However, the dresses served admirably as bundling for our other equipment and provisions, and with Molina's straps and belts, we fashioned ties to make a serviceable pack to secure to Anna's back.

All of this in the dark with hearts and hands quaking. Looking back, I can't imagine how we accomplished it, but we did. Our last challenge would be footwear. Our shoes were not the high-button, heeled creatures that I'd been accustomed to in New York, but the light, thin-soled shoes we wore would last no time at all over the terrain ahead of us. Our main concern now, though, was distance. With Anna in use mainly as a pack animal, we couldn't travel by horseback. And we'd be easy for Santa Anna's experts to track. For the moment, surprise, whatever speed we could manage, and Molina's musket were our only weapons.

We gave one another a hug, a kiss, and a smile, and set out in our underwear to write the first chapter of our story of a journey across the plains.

CHAPTER EIGHTEEN

Nothing Ventured

At dawn we were trudging north, exhausted, but we had to find a way across the river before we dared rest. Santa Anna would have sent trackers after us by now, men able to read our trail as well as a preacher reads a Bible. I wished for rain to wipe out our tracks. Failing that, only crossing the river in a way to cover our trail would put us out of their reach. We found nothing that would pass for a ford, just waters flowing strong and deep between steep and sandy banks.

Colleen finally collapsed, her early optimism dissolving in fatigue and tears. I was afraid that the partner who'd been my savior would become the agent of my defeat. I was terrified, but afraid to show it. My heart pounded as much with fear as with weariness as I pulled at her arm. "Get up, Colleen. I'm not going to let you lie down and quit."

She continued to sob, so I pulled harder on her arm. She got to her knees, then began standing, then slipped and fell, causing me to stumble back, lose my balance, and drop on my rear. She looked up at me, hanging on to her wrist, both of us sprawled there under Santa Anna's nose. I'm sure no one ever gave her a blacker look than the one I sent her way at that moment, but then she did the best thing anyone could have done in that situation. She started laughing. Through tears, mind you, but laughing.

"You look like a rag doll thrown in the yard and forgot about," she said.

I saw no humor in the situation at first, but her giggles overcame my anger, and we were soon in one another's arms, laughing and hugging.

As the laughter faded, our eyes locked on one another, and we shared a silent contemplation of our peril. My mind had shifted to finding ways to cross the river and doing it fast. Not Colleen's.

"We got to pray" is what she said next.

"Are you thinking we can pray our way to San Antonio?" Once again, I feared I'd chosen the wrong partner.

She grabbed my wrist and pulled us shoulder to shoulder on our knees. I'd never been one for church, and to tell the truth, what happened next didn't change me much in that respect. But it did change me somehow even though to this day I couldn't describe just how.

"Our father," Colleen said, looking up at the sky. "Come on, Emily. With me." I had a vague memory of the prayer. Not enough to really join her all the way, but I did my best. "Who art in heaven … Daily bread …Temptation … Evil . . . " I don't know the whole thing even now, but the effect on Colleen of reciting it was lightning.

"Amen," she said. Lowered her eyes and folded my hands in hers, and smiled brighter than I'd ever seen her. "Pontoons," she said.

"Pontoons," I said. "Oh, you mean pontoons like the ones that sunk those cannons on the Brazos?"

"They didn't all go under, now did they? Lots of them made it, and we will too." She placed a hand over her heart. "I know it here. We just need the right log to float us over."

I had no answer to the power of her conviction and no better idea, so I jumped to my feet and pulled her into an embrace. "On with it, then," I said.

We slid down the riverbank, dragging a reluctant Anna behind us. And leaving one great trail for the soldiers chasing us. A powerful eddy ten yards or so upstream from where we landed sent limbs and logs spinning our way, but how to catch and tame one of them without getting bashed to pieces by the others was going to be a problem. I was a pretty good swimmer and somewhat acquainted with the ways of rivers from my time on the Hudson, so I knew that no one should attempt what we had in mind. That was only a minor consideration in our circumstances. It was not if but how.

We rechecked our pack on Anna's back, tightening all the straps, making particularly sure the rifle and bayonet were secure. They would be our only means of replenishing our scant supply of food. Of course neither of them were much good without the gunpowder in Molina's powder horn, and we saw no sure way of keeping it dry. We corked the horn tight, buried it deep inside the pack, and hoped for the best.

The water at our feet was slow and shallow, but I could see there was a dropoff and a strong current a few yards out. We waded out in chilly water, sinking halfway to our knees in the mud, the current pulling at our legs. We managed to snag a small oak that had been pulled out by the roots. Lucky. Any wet log is a slippery log, even with the bark still on it, but having all these roots to hang on to would be a big help.

We waded to the dropoff, tied Anna's rope around a strong-looking limb, and pushed off. Things went badly from the beginning. Anna balked, dug in stiff-legged as we tried to cast off. The current finally pulled her into deep water, but she'd dragged so hard for so long that she forced our log to hug the near bank instead of heading toward the other side. I'd thought we could kick like we were swimming and control our course, but the river and the tree would have none of it. Our "boat" began to turn independent of our efforts. The root end had been pointed upstream when we started, but now was headed downstream, Colleen and I clinging to it with all we had. I couldn't even see Anna.

The current jammed us into some rocks, which crunched my ribs and took my breath. Colleen had plenty of breath though, and she was screaming for help from heaven and earth.

For a minute we were crossways to the current, then the log got pulled into mid-river, and we were suddenly on its upstream end. I could see ahead a ways and was encouraged to see that the river turned left. I thought the chances were good that it would throw us to the right and land us on the other side. It better happen soon, I thought, for it wouldn't be long before we floated right down into the middle of the Mexican army as they crossed over, sending us right into the business end of Santa Anna's whips.

That thought had barely crossed my mind before another crisis topped everything else. Our oak, which had been turning end-to-end, now took a notion to spin around its center. The root I'd been hanging onto pulled me underwater. I had no time to take a breath, clambered wildly in the wet and airless dark, grabbing whatever handholds I could find, trying to pull myself back up. I don't know how long my struggle lasted, how long I scrambled and thrashed, but whatever happened, happened by instinct alone. I must have lost consciousness, for though I recall my chest burning for air, then recall taking my first coughing, sputtering breath above water, what happened in between is blank as a classroom blackboard in summer.

What I saw when I got my bearings brought me near to elation. We were headed straight for a sandbar, where we could land and regroup. We were so far downstream from where we'd entered the water, it would take the army's trackers a long time to figure out where we'd emerged from the river, which would give us time to put some distance between them and us.

"Colleen," I called, "Look. We're going to make it." Silence. "Colleen." I said her name over and over as we continued to float downstream, screaming it, I guess. I neither saw nor heard a response from Colleen, and I saw nothing of Anna either. When we fetched up on the sandbar at last, I threw myself prostrate and dug my fingers into the earth, just for the feeling of having something stable to hang on to. Then I ran back to the tree. There, I discovered why Colleen hadn't answered.

It was her hair that did her in. My partner and friend I'd grown to love hung slumped and lifeless, her tresses snagged in the twigs and roots. She looked like Colleen, but was Colleen no longer. I felt shamed to realize I hadn't understood how deeply I felt about her till that moment, when my love was of no use. Farther downstream, floated Anna, lifeless as Colleen, her corpse moored to the log by the lead rope I'd tied her to when we launched.

It was then I discovered the meaning of grief, what it means for your tears to burn like acid and to choke on your very breath. I've known it many times since, but I've never found a remedy for it. I dropped to my knees, closed my eyes, and did my best to repeat the prayer Colleen and I had said together before we'd begun this disastrous journey. A lot of good that prayer had done her, but she'd needed it then for some reason. Maybe it would do her some good now. And me too.

When I finished and opened my eyes, I panicked to see that the current was reclaiming the log. In a moment I'd lose the supplies in Anna's backpack, and lose the chance to bury my companion. I grabbed her feet, but couldn't hold on. I ran after her. Waded. Swam a few strokes, but all too late.

I stood waist deep in my underwear watching all I had left in the world floating away down the Colorado River.

CHAPTER NINETEEN

Destitute

spent most of the day indulging my misery. It's a fruitless pastime, but the heart cares little about practicality. I found a gully with a small stream and a clump of sagebrush where I curled up and wept. I mourned for Colleen, for Anna. Blamed myself for not loving them better, for risking all of us to this foolish undertaking. I mourned for myself and for my mother, who would never know what had become of me, who would live out her days alone, wondering and wishing. All because I had to have things my way, wasn't willing to be satisfied with my blessings. If I'd had the means and will to commit suicide, I believe I might have done it that day, but I didn't have even that.

I wept myself dry, and when the western sky glowed pink, I did the only thing I could. I got to my feet and started moving North and West, for if I was going to survive, it would be by finding General Houston, and it was in that direction that I'd find his army. If I found it at all.

I trudged through the darkness, the sliver of a new moon giving me no light at all. The spring rains that had left dry creeks with pools of water, or my lack of a vessel for water would have probably done me in. I knew nothing of navigation, could only hope my reading of the moon and the North Star would be enough to guide me.

The moon was low in the eastern sky when I finally succumbed to fatigue. I was sure I hadn't gone far, but just as sure that I couldn't go a step farther. I found another arroyo, another clump of sage, and coiled myself into the warmest ball I could manage. In my stillness, I generated little heat, but managed to shiver my way into a shallow and fretful slumber.

***

The dawn chill, combined with the rain leaking from the gray sky like tears, finally became too much for me to continue wallowing in my misery. I was hungry. The only help for the cold was to get moving, and there was no apparent help for the hunger at all. There was also no apparent help for my shoes. The soles were pulling away from the tops and had thinned to the point where I could feel every pebble. There were a few red and sore spots on my heels that would soon become disabling blisters if I didn't do something. Panic rose in my throat, I closed my eyes and breathed. Our father, I whispered to myself, picturing Colleen at prayer. Poor Colleen. But it calmed me somehow.

My side throbbed from my collision with the rocks the day before, and my tight corset intensified the pain. It was a struggle to loosen the ties without Isabella to help, especially soaked as they were, but I managed, and soon was down to drawers and camisole. No way for a respectable lady to be seen in public, I mused. If you could call this endless plain public.

I'd been bemoaning the rips my drawers and corset had suffered during the struggle with the log. Now I was glad for them. Strange, the things one becomes grateful for in troubled times. The corset's fabric was relatively tough, and I'd have had a difficult time ripping it if not for the slashes that got the process started. I tugged and yanked and employed a sharp stone to cut wrapping strips for my feet. The corset ties served nicely to complete the bindings, which wouldn't last forever but might get me where I was going. And how far was that? Ten miles? Fifty? A hundred? I bundled up what was left of the corset—those stays might still come in handy somehow—and headed out, at my back the vague glow of sun through the clouds.

I'd heard that some plants out here were poisonous, that others would cure anything. Which was which, I couldn't say. However, I couldn't afford not to try a few leaves and berries, both for their moisture and to assuage the hunger pangs. Some were bitter, some heavy with something that puckered me up and sucked the moisture from my mouth. None of them made me sick. Maybe that part would come later. Nice to have something to look forward to. All the time, I watched the southern horizon for signs of the Mexican army, but saw neither dust nor silhouettes. There were moments when I would have welcomed even Toño's company.

The clouds fled, and the sun got warm. Opposite problem. I used the corset remains as a shade, holding it above my head till my arms drained of blood. Once, I saw a lizard on a rock and got the idea of using the corset to trap it for food. If I could just sneak up and throw it over him … I got to within inches before he scooted back under his stone. Pathetic that I'd be reduced to finding a way to make a meal out of a lizard. And failing at that.

Sundown found me in yet another gully, my shoes in tatters, but still holding for the time being. A south wind had picked up, and a fresh contingent of clouds slouched its way north. There'd been no rain for a few days, but it appeared that was about to change. It could be a wet night.

No blisters—yet. No Mexican Army—yet. However, except for the occasional leaves and berries, I hadn't eaten for two days. How long before I'd get not just uncomfortable, but weak? I ignored those questions, ignored my fear, fought down my sobs, and focused on the next step. And the next. And the next.

***

It was around noon the next day, muddy and wet, when I stumbled.

I'd been skirting a dry wash, afraid for the fear of flash floods, to climb down into it then out the other side. Close to the edge, two things happened at once. The mud took my feet from under me, and the bank collapsed. Then came the landslide that followed me down the bank and the falling rock that bounced against my skull.

The sun, barely discernable behind the clouds, was midway to the horizon when I awoke, my head a balloon of pain ready to explode. I felt blood running from behind my ear and down my cheek over my jaw and on to my chest. I pushed myself to my feet, but shouted in agony when I tried to put weight on my right ankle. I recalled thinking back in the camp that a sprained ankle could finish Coleen and my escape. Colleen's finish had involved more than that, but apparently that's all it was going to take for me.

The best I could hope for now was that Santa Anna's men would succeed in tracking me down. I whimpered my way into unconsciousness, sure that my flight was over, one way or another.

I awoke to a shove in the back and a command I didn't understand. Then another helping of both. I turned my head in dizzy anguish and beheld one of the most welcome—and most terrifying—sights I'd ever seen. Above me hovered two Indian braves, clothed in breechclouts and feathers and paint. They both carried war clubs, but they hadn't used them on me. Maybe they wouldn't. Or wouldn't till later. After … I reached out my hand.

"Help me, please. I'm hurt."

CHAPTER TWENTY

Rescued?
March 09, 1836

"**I** am Chief Bowl."

From my kneeling position, I tried to lift my throbbing head and bring into focus the man towering over me. I made out that he was broad-shouldered and dressed in a feathered cloak and a breechclout. I opened my mouth to reply, but the effort set my brain spinning, and I tipped to the right and blacked out.

I awoke choking and coughing. My head was wet, and someone had poured water into my mouth. Rough hands pulled me out of mud back to my knees.

"Who are you?" The same voice. I kept my eyes to the ground this time, narrowed my attention to the chief's beaded moccasins and the chill of the breeze, afraid that trying to take in more would send me reeling again.

"Emily," I mumbled. "West." More water splashed against the spot where the rock had crashed into my head. I gasped, reached toward the wound. Another rough hand, or perhaps the same one, pulled my hand down.

"Later," the man said to whoever had grabbed me. He turned his attention back to me. "Not your name only. Tell why you are here."

Such a long story. I knew I could never get through it in my present state. But if I didn't satisfy this man, how much worse awaited me? A vision of Colleen floating down the Colorado drifted through my mind, the cries of the men Santa Anna had flogged. A warmth dribbled down my cheek. I was bleeding again. Terror flooded my heart. Tears began. I couldn't afford them here if it was true what I'd heard that Indians valued fortitude above all. I reached back for some comforting word from my mother, but nothing she'd said had prepared me for this. I'd heard Houston had friends among some Indians. I prayed what I'd heard was true, and that these were his Indians.

"General Houston," I said.

Suddenly, the chief dropped to my level, lifted my chin to meet his eyes. "What of Houston?" he said. Eyes are supposed to be the window to the soul, but Chief Bowl's windows had been painted over. I couldn't divine either from his voice or his face whether his question was hopeful or hostile.

"Take me there," I said. "To him."

He grabbed my hair, yanked my head back. "Dark skin. Hair that curls. Are you his slave?"

I was dizzy again. What was the right answer? I spoke before deciding what I was going to say. "Friend," I said. "Good friend."

The chief with the strange name released my hair, stood and laughed. Others around him laughed as well, though judging by the two warriors who had found me, I doubted most of them could have followed the English conversation. He barked out some orders. Women lifted me to my feet, supporting me under the shoulders as we stumbled through the makeshift village toward a distant lean-to. I could tell I had an audience for my procession and became conscious of my immodest dress. Yet my escorts wore nothing at all above the waist, so by civilized standards I was better clothed than they were.

I stumbled over a rock, nearly tumbled, but the women were strong and dragged me along without much effort. Before long, I was reclining on a pallet of branches and reeds, covered with a deerhide blanket, and I gave myself over to an exhausted sleep.

***

I thought Santa Anna was on top of me, pressing on me, holding me down. I tried to turn over. Tried and tried, but I couldn't move. Get off me, damn your ugly eyes. Off. I got no response from the general, but heard plenty of female chatter in a language I didn't understand. Not Spanish.

I came back to myself slowly, trying to remember what had happened, to figure out what was going on. The reason I couldn't move was that I lay strapped down. But the restraints weren't to imprison or punish me. They kept me from sliding off the travois, a rawhide hammock slung between wooden poles and dragged behind a horse. The travois poles gouged ditches in the mud behind us as we progressed. It wasn't raining at that moment, but the dampness of my dress was evidence that it had and would. It was a rocky, slippery ride and would have been a perilous one if not for the ties. A poultice of some sort covered the wound on my head. I smelled strongly of sage and could feel the grease of salves all over my arms and face. Doubtless over my whole body. The women had clothed me in a plain deerskin dress. I smelled of rancid grease and woodsmoke. I wondered what had happened to my underwear.

I was thankful for this Chief Bowl's help, thankful for a clear head and that I felt neither hungry nor thirsty. But I also hated lying helpless and useless.

"Bowl," I yelled. Or intended to yell, but my voice sounded weak to my ears, and it attracted no attention as far as I could see. I tried again, with the same result. The third time, I took a full breath, closed my eyes and screamed. It sounded louder than my earlier plea, though not up to my healthy volume. Still, it got a response. The horse stopped, and the travois stilled. A woman my mother's age appeared by my side, said something I couldn't understand. She wore the same kind of dress I did. Perhaps they covered themselves for protection when they traveled. A foolish thing to reflect on in my present situation.

I raised my head, an action that did not dizzy me this time. Attempting to appear strong, I tried to smile. Maybe I succeeded. "Bowl," I said. "Chief Bowl." The woman grunted, walked away, and the travois began moving once again.

The effort had exhausted me. I laid my head down and closed my eyes. I didn't fall asleep, though, so I knew I was better. How much better? I'd have to get off the damn stretcher to find out.

"Hey," I called as loud as I could. It sounded louder to me this time, though I was no judge. Regardless, I had to keep it up till I got some help. "I need to see Chief Bowl. Bowl. Bowl. Now." I interspersed my yelling with periods of rest. After several rounds of this, the horse finally stopped again and Bowl appeared beside me.

He wore no feathers this time. And no paint. I hadn't recalled that his face was painted when first we met until I saw him without it. A measure of how weak I'd been. Warriors and women stood close behind him. The men might have been the same ones who rescued me, but I couldn't be sure. The aroma of unwashed bodies floated over the scene.

"Curled hair friend of General Houston," he said. "You have returned."

"How long have I been unconscious?" I said.

"We must talk," he said. He hadn't answered my question. Disconcerting, but I was to find it was one of his ways. I decided not to respond directly to him either. This subtle defiance is one of my ways, another signal that my health was returning.

"I can walk," I said.

He cocked his head as if skeptical. "We shall see." He nodded, and the woman who had appeared earlier untied my bonds and stepped back. Bowl signaled to me to rise, which I did. It took me a moment to stand without leaning against the travois poles. I looked around, and it seemed the whole tribe was waiting on me, watching. Several other travois, mounted warriors, women with bundles on their backs, naked children with sticks in their hands. It had begun raining again and the breeze picked up. None of them made an effort to cover up or paid attention to it in any other way. In another moment I'd completed a few tentative steps, and before long I was walking almost normally. I stepped off in the direction the tribe had been moving, and put on the bravest front I could manage. I even waved to Chief Bowl to catch up with me.

"Let's go," I said.

He, in turn, pointed forward, and the procession advanced. I now focused on the road ahead instead of on myself. Bowl trotted to my side, laid a hand on my shoulder.

"We will ride," he said. In short order, we were both mounted. I was accustomed to riding astride, but the horsehair felt rough, though not unpleasant, against my bare bottom, and adjusting to the lack of stirrups took a while. We trotted to what must have been Bowl's customary place at the head of the column. The trotting set my head to throbbing, but I did not feel dizzy, so I tightened my jaws and said nothing. Soon, we slowed to a more comfortable pace.

"You will tell me more now, friend of Houston," he said.

"Emily," I said. "You can call me Emily, please."

"How is it you are friend to Houston?"

"We met at Morgan's Point. Do you know it?" Silence. I would have to go on without a clue as to what he was looking to find out. Did he know the General, or did he merely know who he was? Either way, did he consider a friend of the General a friend of his, or an enemy? What if I misspoke? Perhaps if I kept my explanation vague. "He asked for my help," I said. "I obliged him. We talked. Many times."

"And the help?" he said. "What was it?" He was not going to let me off so lightly. I decided to try skipping the whole interrogation, to try getting the answers to my own questions about the relationship between Bowl and Houston in one fell swoop.

"Take me to him," I said. "Let him tell you himself."

The chief looked for the briefest instance startled. It's not often, I was to learn, that you catch him looking vulnerable even for that long. Then his look hardened.

He made one of his imperious gestures. A mounted warrior appeared beside me, grabbed the rope of my hackamore and turned me toward the rear of the procession. We soon arrived at the same horse-and-travois outfit I had left a short time earlier. He motioned me to dismount. I obeyed. The woman who led the horse that pulled the travois paid no attention to any of it, just kept tramping along with the rest of the convoy. One minute I was riding beside the chief, leading everyone. The next, I was afoot and trudging through the mud with the other women. At least they'd given me a sturdy pair of moccasins, and I wasn't lost. I wished, though, I had the faintest idea where we were going.

CHAPTER TWENTY-ONE

Gonzales

I thought we'd left rivers behind us when I landed on the west bank of the Colorado and watched Colleen's body float downstream. Between the Brazos and the Colorado, I'd had quite enough of these uncivilized waters, so different from my beloved Hudson with its green-wooded banks and its waterways filled with sails and steamboats. Nothing I'd ever seen afloat—even the Indians' canoes—would last any time at all in these wild torrents. And yet, here we came, smack up against another stream. The Indians called it a name I couldn't understand. I learned later that Mexicans and whites alike called it the Guadalupe.

It was no more navigable than the other two rivers, even swollen by the recent rains, but not because of its raging current. Rather because it was so small and tame, at least where we encountered it. Still, the thought of crossing any river at all made a fist of my stomach. I need not have feared, however, for instead of crossing, we turned straight north and followed a trail along its east bank. The land turned from just muddy to wet and green. We began to see cattle in the distance. Then the Apaches appeared on our right flank.

At first, they presented themselves as a mounted picket line on a hill ahead of us, then the line increased in numbers southward, every one of them armed with spears and rifles, their very presence menacing, as if they'd swoop down on us and drive us into the river. I changed my mind about the crossing then, thinking it would be good to have the Guadalupe between us and them.

Bowl had stopped our procession an hour or so before we saw them, ordered us into a defensive posture in a grove of cottonwoods. I'd had no idea why at the time. Nor did I know the intruders by the name "Apache" until later, though I guessed these might be from that fearsome tribe. I surmised that Bowl's scouts had seen the approaching warriors and that he was preparing us to meet them.

What a place is this Texas, I thought to myself. Everywhere you turn, some savage enemy or another is out to get you. Dr. Morgan had neglected to include the word "slaughterhouse" in the contract I'd signed. I might have already been laid on the chopping block if I hadn't mentioned Houston's name when I first met Bowl. I might be laid there yet if the Apaches got the best of us. Suddenly, for the hundredth time since the Colorado, I missed Colleen. I'd at least have someone to talk to about my fear. Even a Spanish speaker would do. I could stumble along with a few words and some sign language. But all I had acquired of what turned out to be Chief Bowl's language of Cherokee were a few random words like "fire," "meat," "beans." Useless for the current situation. I was reduced to frightful watching and guessing.

My group of women crouched behind an improvised breastwork of piled driftwood and downed branches. We had knives, and several women had whittled long sticks to points. Two brandished bows and arrows. The women were enthusiastic and talking tough, but if it came to combat, our prospects were meager. I figured we could fend off an attack by half-dozen boys, women, or old men. More than that, and we'd better be ready to swim.

Nothing happened for a long time. Casual thunderheads floated through a sunny sky while we hunkered down behind our little stockade, and I now watched the cottonwood shadows lengthen, inching eastward toward the warriors sitting skylined on their horses. None of the other women seemed bothered, as if what we were doing was normal. My mother would have said it was a lesson in patience, and good for me. It was a lesson I'd had many times but somehow the skill had escaped me.

I whittled myself a spear. I tried to plot the best route across the river. The bank directly opposite was steep and sandy as far downstream as I could see. I decided that upstream to a small beach fifty or so yards away was my best bet. The current appeared sluggish, though I knew that could be deceptive, but there were lots of roots and branches to hang on to. I could pull myself upstream by those if necessary. My progress would be slow, and I'd be exposed till I reached my landing. Still, if it came to that, I'd gotten pretty good as a girl at holding my breath underwater.

And what if I did land safely? We'd been headed north, and it seemed Bowl genuinely intended to meet my General. He must be near, or at least Bowl thought so. I'd just walk upstream and hope for the best. I was in the middle of imagining how my meeting with Houston might go when the women started to chatter and point.

Three warriors, bequilled with feathers and weapons galloped toward the enemy lines. After they'd ridden a hundred yards or so, they raised lances and began whooping. After another fifty yards, the whooping unabated, they circled their horses, then one after the other thrust their spears into the earth. They stopped whooping then and stilled their horses behind the lances, facing the Apaches. They stood there for another couple of minutes, then wheeled about and galloped back in our direction.

More waiting. Shadows continued to lengthen. The sky began to redden behind us. Then the Apaches moved, or at least five of them did. They walked their ponies toward our lances. Once there, they thrust their own lances into the ground just east of those the Cherokees had planted. However, they did not withdraw. Instead, they formed a sort of honor guard—two columns facing each other—and another of the Apaches rode toward them. I figured he must be the head man, though he wasn't more elaborately adorned than the others.

We women remained still, entranced, till nearby hoofbeats

interrupted us. One of Bowl's warriors dashed into our little compound. He pointed his lance at me. The other women withdrew, leaving me to face the horseman alone. He slapped his horse's haunch, jerked his chin in a motion that seemed so suggest I should jump aboard and ride away with him like a trick rider in a circus. I was paralyzed with fright and puzzlement. His repeated gestures grew more intense and rapid. Two women pushed me toward him. Finally, I reached out an arm, and he pulled me on to the horse as if I weighed no more than a barnyard hen, and we galloped away.

The ride was swift and brief, so brief I couldn't even formulate questions to myself. In an instant, I was amazed to find myself standing in front of Bowl for the first time since he'd dismissed me to walking by my travois.

"You will come with us, Emily West," he said. He gestured, a warrior walked a horse forward, and Bowl himself boosted me aboard. Shortly, I found myself riding beside Bowl, followed by three painted and armed warriors, and we went forth, apparently to meet Bowl's Apache counterpart. Was this a parley or a preface to battle? And what was I doing here? If they were counting on me to wield a musket or a bow and arrow, they were in for a disappointment.

The ceremony at the lances took a long time. There were speeches. Circling. Dismounting, Mounting. Bowing in four directions. Goods— rifles, hatchets, knives, beads—exchanged hands. It was during that part of the activities that I developed a theory—became convinced, actually—about my part in the show. My stomach lurched near to vomiting at the notion that Bowl was using me to purchase safe passage through Apache territory.

I maneuvered my horse close to his.

"You'll have to kill me," I said in a low voice. "I won't go."

He didn't respond, didn't even look at me. Just made another of those small gestures, and I found myself braced by a pair of his warriors, braced so tightly neither my horse nor I stood a chance of moving, which didn't do my nausea any good. I swallowed bile and tried to prepare myself.

Bowl spoke a while. Then my escorts nudged me forward. Bowl spoke some more, gesturing toward me often. I heard Houston's name mentioned a couple of times. The Apaches became agitated, their voices rose. Their ponies shifted and turned. Finally one of them charged toward me, grabbed my hackamore, and tried to pull me toward their side. I screamed, spit at him, and yanked back on the rope. Neither my expectoration nor my feeble jerk on the rope had the least effect. Not so, the blow from one of Bowl's warriors—the butt of his lance to the temple—which slammed my attacker to the ground. A second warrior thrust a lance into the earth within an inch of the warrior's throat.

Things got quiet after that. The Apache chief stood still a while, then turned his horse and rode east, followed by his troops. His downed soldier struggled to his feet and followed them at a trot, falling ever farther behind until he disappeared over the hill. Apparently, his companions had left him horseless as punishment, either for his brashness or for his lack of success at wresting me from the Cherokees.

My two escorts guided me at a good pace back to the women's compound, waited till I dismounted, then left me where I'd started. Retelling it, it seems I should have been relieved considering that I'd escaped what I thought would be slavery or even death. Instead, I stood amazed, mystified, and bewildered, understanding almost nothing of what had happened.

And no one was about to explain it to me, even if they'd been able. Someone thrust some jerky into my hand, and we hastily packed up for what proved to be a night march. Judging by the grumbling and outright fear among my companions, this was unusual. But orders, it seemed, were orders, and we went on our new-moon way. The thunderheads joined forces to hide that feeble moon and to send torrents upon us. Still, we marched.

When Bowl finally ordered a halt, we didn't bother with our normal camping ritual of fires and temporary shelters. Instead, we watered and hobbled the horses, chewed on some more jerky, threw down some bedding and collapsed in the mud.

Sunrise roused us. The sky had turned brilliant as if it had never heard of such a thing as a storm. I wondered how far we'd have to march today, but I was surprised to see preparations beginning for what appeared would be a substantial stay—rocks for fire sites. Teepees. Horses organized into remudas. Because of the dark, I'd missed the fact the countryside had greened considerably. The occasional cattle we'd seen from afar further south wandered in herds here in the near distance.

I ignored for the moment my filthy clothing and the other chores that awaited me and the others and walked toward a gathering on a nearby rise, and when I reached it, I was overjoyed to see that we were gazing on a town. A prosperous community with the closest things to mansions and estates I'd seen since I left the east coast.

Bowl was standing there with a number of his men. He appeared happy to see me, invited me to stand beside him. His change of attitude gladdened me, then made me suspicious. I was beginning to live a life governed by fear, and I didn't much like it.

"This is Gonzales, Emily West," he said. "You have proved useful to us."

I didn't know what he meant, but decided to act as if I understood all that had gone on the previous day. "Glad to be of service, Chief Bowl," I said. I was tempted to curtsy, but resisted. "I'm sure you'll let me know if there's anything else I can do."

Did he smile? Probably my imagination. "Perhaps Houston will meet us here, and we can hear from his own lips about the help you say you gave him."

Would the General back up my story? And if he didn't? I was about to find out.

CHAPTER TWENTY-TWO

Reunion

Three days we camped outside of Gonzales. Our diet improved considerably augmented by beef from the surrounding herds. The Indians got some firewater from some place, and the evenings became filled with whoops and dancing and warrior games. I don't know to this day why the Cherokees suffered no repercussions for killing the local cattle, but I fell on the meat with gusto. I'd lost so much weight during the trek that I felt rather emaciated. I certainly wouldn't have filled out the bodice that tempted the patrons at Morgan's hotel.

And I worried about the future. What had become of the poke I'd entrusted to Houston's care, albeit without his knowledge? If he didn't show up, would I become an Indian slave? Would I, could I, flee again? And to where this time? Back to Santa Anna? Into the arms of the Apaches?

While I worried, tried to form plans, I became one of the tribal women doing tribal women's chores. Gathering wood. Scraping hides of the slaughtered cattle. Tending fires. I didn't mind the work, but it was lonely, being treated like the outsider I was, knowing so little of the language. Even though I picked up more words, learned some phrases, I still had no one to talk with, no one with whom to share my feelings, fears, plans. I had been on my own before, but never isolated like this. I think people who live alone inside themselves are living in a dangerous place. It's rather like cannibalizing yourself when you keep chewing on your own emotions and ideas over and over, nothing from the outside to nourish them. So, even though I had beefsteak to feed my body, my heart and soul languished.

At dawn on the fourth day, I stood alone on the hill where I'd first joined Bowl when we'd arrived at Gonzales. Bright as the rising sun was, my thoughts had turned dark. I'd been contemplating a trip into town. There were English speakers there certainly, and even with my elementary Spanish I could communicate with some Mexicans. I had skills and experience enough to support myself, to try to earn passage back to New York, or at least to Morgan's Point where my employer would help. All these fantasies, though, seemed futile, vanished in the flames that had consumed my contract at Santa Anna's supper table. Without those papers, any slave trader—and I'd encountered a few even at Morgan's point—could grab me and deliver me for cash to the nearest cotton plantation. I'd be better off with the Indians.

I heard a call from one of the women. I knew they wanted me to fetch water, and I resigned myself to the chore, turned, then something appeared in the distance. No more than a dot of ink on a blotter, but it hadn't been there a moment earlier. Others saw it as well, and so cries erupted from sentries stationed on other hilltops. Suddenly no one seemed to care about water or wood. The hillsides filled with spectators as a large procession materialized out of the dust like specters from a mist. The closer they came, the more apparent it became that we were watching an army on the march. They weren't slick and polished regiments like Santa Anna's *soldados*. There were a few uniforms, but mostly the troops looked like backwoodsmen pulled off their homesteads. Though the men didn't march in rank and file, they all carried weapons. Mules pulled a few cannon as well as supply wagons. And at the head rode a man I recognized both by his stature and by his distinctive fringed buckskins. I wondered if they'd been washed since I'd laundered them myself those weeks earlier.

I resisted the urge to rush down the hill, knowing that I'd have to follow some sort of protocol, but confident from Bowl's comments that I was destined to meet Houston face-to-face soon. I turned to the woman standing next to me, hugged her tight, and kissed her forehead. Startled and surprised, she started to push me away, then—seeing my smile, I suppose—smiled herself and hugged me back. My first overt gesture of affection since I'd joined Chief Bowl's tribe. For a moment, I missed Colleen, Mother, and the whole life I'd left behind. But in the next moment, my heart filled with hope and anticipation for what was to come now that General Houston had returned.

***

The council took place the following evening outside Houston's tent. His dress embodied the contrast between Santa Anna's army and that of the Texicans, as they called themselves now. No shiny buttons or epaulettes. Not even a military hat. On a street, you'd have perhaps been impressed by his stature and piercing eyes, but you wouldn't have picked him out as a soldier, let alone as a general. Nor would you have described that gathering as a meeting of high level officials.

The general sat in a bentwood chair with Deef Smith and a couple of lieutenants I didn't know standing beside him. Chief Bowl sat opposite with a few warriors standing in positions similar to Houston's minions. There had been some ceremony—a pipe, a few words—before they sat. However, Houston seemed impatient with all that, anxious to get to the conversation at hand. I stood back, behind Bowl in a group of lesser warriors, the only female in attendance. Houston had spotted me and nodded, but that had been the only acknowledgement he'd offered. I nodded back in kind. No smile, assuming that a deadpan expression was the order of the day and determined not to disrupt procedures.

"We have not met since you became General," Bowl said. "And it is said you are now the leader of something they call a republic."

"And it has been too long since we offered our hands to one another as brothers, Bowl," Houston answered. "What you have heard is true. We have determined to free our people from the tyranny of their oppressors and to free your people as well. Together, we can become a nation recognized and respected by all nations in the world."

"Ah, but the Napoleon of the West. He is a great obstacle, is he not?"

"Indeed he is."

"And your men. Compared to his, they are few and poor."

"They appear so, yes. But that is part of our strength. Santa Anna is prideful and overconfident. We may have fewer soldiers, but we are mighty in spirit and in cunning."

"Forgive me, General, if I say that your words appear to be something of a boast."

"Ah, but you perhaps forget, Chief, that twice—under General Washington and later under General Jackson—Americans with fewer men and weapons sent the great British stampeding home in defeat. And that Napoleon himself died alone on an Island no bigger than our own Galveston on the shores of Texas. We are confident of victory."

"With such confidence, then, you have no need of Bowl."

"Again, there is more at work here than is apparent, both for our people and for yours. First, with Cherokee help, our victory will come sooner and with less cost in men and goods and enable the Republic to prosper immediately. Second, I alone am not the Republic. I cannot emphasize enough how much easier it will be to gather support for the good of your people from our other leaders if you have a hand in our victory."

"And how much harsher it will be for us if there is defeat instead."

Houston stood, spread his arms. "There can be no defeat, Chief Bowl. The government we formed in Washington-on-the-Brazos is now the Republic of Texas and will soon become the power of this territory. No matter what, you and I will be brothers for all our lives. However, as comrades in arms, our nations will be united as well. Tell me you'll join us."

Bowl stood and extended his arm. The two men grasped each

other's forearms, looked into one another's eyes. "I cannot command this, Houston," he said.

"But you can recommend. To your council."

"And I shall."

"And soon. The Alamo awaits."

Another moment of eye contact. They dropped their hands. The business appeared concluded for the time being, and Houston gestured toward me. "I see you have someone in your retinue with whom I am acquainted."

Bowl, in his usual way, ordered me forward with a movement of his hand that amounted to no more than a twitch.

"Emily West tells me she knows you."

"Indeed she does." He smiled. "We met at Morgan's Point, where she served me well. In a number of ways." He winked.

I was overjoyed that Houston had confirmed my story about helping him out, even though I was not particularly happy with the salacious implications behind the manner of his words and the winking.

"I am very glad to see you again, Miss West." He opened his arms.

An embrace in other circumstances might have been an overstep. We had never touched each other even to shake hands. But here, deprived as I'd been of human contact with someone of my own kind—or closer to it than anyone I'd met in what seemed like years—I rushed into his arms like a long-lost lover. I remembered how I'd spilled beer on him the first time we'd met. Then hot water. Now I was spilling tears. It was a struggle not to break down in sobs, but I knew this was neither the time nor place. I wondered if would ever have such a time or place. He grasped my shoulders gently and pushed me back. Much as I wanted to hold on tight, I relinquished my embrace without protest.

"Well, well, Miss Emily West," he said, his voice an affectionate rumble, "however did you wind up here and dressed like a heathen, too?"

"General Houston. Sir. Please take me with you." I looked in his eyes, shook my head, trying to say that I couldn't explain right then. "Please."

"Well, I'm not necessarily opposed, Miss Emily," he said. "But I reckon Chief Bowl might have on opinion on the matter."

"No. No. Don't even ask him."

"Did he mistreat you?"

Why I hesitated, I'm not sure. Perhaps because I'd been so miserable with the Cherokee, but put to me directly, I couldn't think of a single instance of real cruelty. "No," I said finally. "In fact, he saved my life, and the Cherokees have been generous to me by their lights. But I don't belong with them. I belong with you and your people. He has no need of me."

"Deef," Houston called. "Would you see that someone brings Miss Emily here a drink of water and a bite of some white man's food. Maybe a hunk of corn pone or something. Chief Bowl and I have some more business."

"Yes, sir, General," Smith said. He sounded obedient, but the sour look he cast in my direction almost made me wish myself back with the Indians.

Bowl and his warriors were standing by their horses, clearly ready to leave, waiting for Houston to say his good-byes. The two leaders stepped away for a private word, a conversation of which I could hear not a word, though it was certainly about me. Houston, as usual, spoke volumes with his hands. Even when he was silent, they were always busy, usually with whittling, while the mulled things over. What was taking so long?

A scruffy looking boy of no more than sixteen brought me a canteen and a hunk of corn bread I could no more have eaten than I could have eaten a cotton boll at that point. I took a sip of water and smilingly gave him the food. He seemed overjoyed to get it. Houston's soldiers were apparently traveling on short rations.

Finally, Bowl turned away from Houston and walked back to his horse. He leaped aboard, waved at me, then loped away with his retinue. My rescue was complete.

I ran to Houston and leaped back into his arms. "Thank you," I cried. "I thought I would never be safe again." This time, he allowed the embrace to last only a few seconds, but lifted me off my feet and set me down at arm's length.

"You better understand something, Emily West. You are no more safe than a plump chicken at supper time. You have just joined an army on its way to war."

CHAPTER TWENTY-THREE

Military Intelligence

As we watched the Cherokees head out, Smith asked, "They going to help us or not, General?"

"Maybe, but most likely not unless the Apaches team up with the pepperbellies. The redskins understand the idea of balance of power as well as any European prime minister."

"Well, I don't know what Europe's got to do with it, but we sure as hell don't want to go up against the Apaches and the Mexicans together."

A sarcastic remark about Deef's ignorance leapt to mind, but I bit my tongue and waited to see what the General would say.

"Right as usual, Deef," he said. "So let's just carry on with our fingers crossed. Tell Big Foot Wallace to spend the afternoon drilling the troops, then have everyone to rest up as best they can tonight. We'll cross the river tomorrow, then it's on to San Antonio to rescue our boys holding out at the Alamo. You cross over now with Karnes and Hardy and scout ahead, make sure no ambush is waiting for us."

"Yessir, Sam. Er … General." And Smith disappeared into the crowd.

And some crowd it was. In addition to the ragtag troops, there were plenty of women and children gathered around makeshift fires. It looked more like a flock of refugees than a fighting army. The General read my question before I asked it.

"I wonder if Napoleon had to deal with a crowd of civilians as well as his soldiers," he said.

"What are they doing here? Don't they know Santa Anna's liable to attack?"

"Sure they do. But they figure they're better off here than on their homesteads where the Mexican soldiers or the Apaches might burn them out any time."

"But you said the Apaches—"

"Apaches don't need a declaration of war to kill settlers. And Santa Anna's copying Napoleon's scorched earth tactic. Leave no shelter or crops or livestock that might benefit our army."

"I can tell you how much he loves the sound of that 'Napoleon of the West' title someone dreamed up for him."

"Yeah, well, I love the sound of the word 'Waterloo.' But right now I'm parched and starved. Let's eat. My quarters. My treat."

So once again, I was on my way to a General's tent for a meal. I hoped with quite different results than the last time.

***

And different it was from start to finish. There was no elegant service, no long table. Just folding camp stools that didn't match the folding table which was barely large enough for one, let alone two. The same youngster to whom I'd given my cornbread plopped down metal plates with beans and more cornbread in front of us.

"Coffee coming up, General," he said.

"Thanks, Zachary." Houston said.

I expressed my own gratitude, realized how my appetite had grown now that I was free from both the Mexicans and the Indians. I looked around briefly for a spoon, then decided I might as well use my fingers as I'd been doing with the Indians all this time anyhow. Houston noted my confusion.

"Here, here take mine," he said. "I'll have Zach bring me one."

He pulled a teaspoon out of some inner pocket, wiped it on his sleeve, and passed it over. I wondered if my fingers might have been cleaner, but decided not to contest the matter and started to shovel the beans into my mouth. They were barely done enough to chew, but delicious still. Zach rushed in with Houston's utensil, and he fell to as well. Our beverage was water in a canteen we passed back and forth.

"As soon as you can, I want to hear it all," he said.

I started to ask all what, but realized it was a silly question, The first two or three mouthfuls, took the edge off my hunger, so I slowed down on the eating and began my story. Over beans, cornbread and water in those simple surroundings I told him everything.

I always hold back part of myself in such situations, like a general holding a squad or two in reserve to send in if the battle starts to move the enemy's way. Facts, yes. Feelings, no. I always felt that to reveal my emotions in a fell swoop left me too vulnerable. But the more I told that afternoon, the less I was able to stop myself. In the days and weeks of isolation that had made it imperative for me to hide my pain and terror the emotional pressure had built in me like a geyser, ready to erupt, and erupt I did.

Santa Anna's abuse, my past loves, our escape, Colleen's body splayed like a female Christ against the roots of that tree, the Apache warrior's grip. Houston's eyes widened, then narrowed to slits as he listened. He didn't stop me. Just passed me the canteen from time to time. Thinking back, I don't think I was long by the clock in the telling, but I packed a great deal of action into every second. By the end, tears streamed down my cheeks, but I was neither sobbing nor whining. In fact, I think I was smiling. Sort of.

"So here I am," I said. "At last."

"Damned shame," he said. At first I thought he was talking about me. But then he said. "We could have done with those cap and ball rifles, and now they're going to be used against us."

"Spoken like a general," I said. I stood and turned away.

"But not like much of a man, Emily. I'm sorry. Come here." We stepped toward one another, and he guided me to his cot, where he rocked me in his arms while, at last, I did sob and whine to a high degree. He indulged me this way for as long as he could bear it, I suppose, which didn't seem long to me. Then he took my arms, straightened me, looked in my eyes, and smiled. They were so blue, those eyes, and I was to love looking into them more and more each day in the weeks ahead.

"Would you like it back now?" he said.

I had only a moment of confusion before I realized what he was talking about. "I thought it was safer to leave my savings with you than to take it on those wagons," I said. "I guess I was right."

"You might have warned me."

"You remember the night I prepared your bath." It wasn't a question. He nodded. "You left your own bag of coins where I could easily have filched a few." He nodded. "And you left it there not by accident."

"No," he said. "Not by accident."

"I figured after that, we were meant to place our trust in one another," I said.

"You're lucky no one offered up a new batch of rifles," he said, "or I might have been tempted."

"I'd be honored for you to keep my little nest egg for a while longer, General. I can think of no safer place." I kissed my first two fingers and placed them on his brow. "Thank you."

He placed his own fingers where I had left the kiss, smiled, stood, and offered me his hands. "Now, Emily West, let's take a walk and get down to business." He guided me out of the tent into the campground. "Leaving your personal troubles out of it, I want you to tell me everything you observed about Santa Anna's army. How many troops. How many guns. How many horses and mules. What kind of training he gave them."

As we walked, we carried on a conversation laden with military matters, but on the way he spoke to his men—soldiers and civilians alike.

"Afternoon, General. What's the word from the Alamo?"

"They're holding out, Jillian. Say a prayer for them. Brave men all."

"God bless you, General Houston."

"God bless our new republic, Jillian. You just keep that beef stew of yours coming so our men are fit to give those Mexicans what they deserve."

"Got a fresh pot boiling right over there, General."

"Amen."

From an improvised parade ground in the near distance came a cry of Column left. Column right. No. No. Right Dagnab it. Right. Zeke. Better Better."

Houston pointed to a man with a booming bass voice who was giving the orders. "Big Foot Wallace. He has a job. These pioneers see no point in all this drill, drill, drill. They're used to hunting possum and bear and 'coons. Want to just run out and start shooting whatever they see whenever they see it. The idea of getting organized and hitting the enemy all together at the right time and place to make the biggest impact? Might as well send them to a full dress ball."

And the rag tag group fit the General's description exactly. They were every age and race imaginable. Unlike Santa Anna's troops, who drilled in unison, shoulders back, chins high, with crisp precision, the Texicans slouched their way reluctantly through the movements. Their musket barrels pointed every which way, like an untended coiffure. How this so-called army was to defeat Santa Anna and save the Alamo or anything else was beyond my ken. The idea would have been laughable had not my very life depended on the outcome.

Houston must have read my thoughts, for he steered me away from the parade ground and resumed his conversation about my time with that other general.

"In those romantic interludes you had with Santa Anna, did he receive dispatches?"

"Sometimes."

"So he allowed business to interrupt his … dalliance."

"Occasionally. But not nearly enough, in my opinion."

"Even with you. Hard to fathom, Emily."

"Isn't it though?" I gave him a smile. "But it happened nevertheless."

He shook his head, a twinkle in his eye. "And did these dispatches come in a pouch or merely tucked in a messenger's tunic?"

"What difference would that make, General?"

"To the dalliance, probably nothing, though you'd be the better judge of that. But to the messages a great deal if they're scribbling notes without bothering to holster them or seal them properly it could be a sign of haste and disorganization."

"I never saw such a pouch."

"Was he hasty in other matters?"

"Not a proper question, General … "

"Granted," he said. "I'm liable to come up with those from time to time."

"Oh?" I said, both fearful and intrigued about what might come next.

"Like I might even ask if you'd care for a peek inside my tent."

"That might start people talking," I said.

"So?" he answered. "I am the general after all."

I hesitated, looked around to see if anyone was watching. It was dark enough to suppose that the twilight might hide us. "Well," I said. "I suppose a good soldier should always follow the general's orders."

"Don't consider it an order," he said. He pulled back the canvas that covered the entrance to the tent. "More in the way of an invitation."

I looked around again. He winked. I smiled. We stepped inside, and he let the tent flap close behind us.

CHAPTER TWENTY-FOUR

Black, White, Yellow

Sweetness slipped out of the bed, her feet silent on the earthen floor of the tent. I could hear her pour water and then caught the sharp smell of coarsely ground coffee spooned into the pot. The pot clanked against the makeshift grill over the small fire pit. It would only take a few minutes before the aroma of brewing coffee would fill the tent.

"Sam. It's time to wake up."

It was still dark, but as the leader, I was charged to be first up and out, and I couldn't pretend sleep any longer so I rolled over to watch her slather several pieces of bread with butter topped by grape jelly from the wild mustang fruit that covered the scrub forest. Not only was this land flowing with milk and honey, but you couldn't beat mustang grape jam or dewberries as big as your thumb.

She used the hem of her gown as a heat pad to lift the pot and tilt the bottom.

She put a tray—nothing but a raw board, really—on the bed, then put the breakfast treat on it before she fetched the coffee, carrying a cup in each hand.

"That's a feast fit for a king, not to mention the sumptuous banquet last night."

She smiled shyly. Always, when private matters between a man and a woman were broached, she demurred. She handed me a mug.

"Just black."

"Black and strong, like I like my women." She cringed as my body turned hot with shame. My heart pounded as I sputtered, "No. No, that's not what I meant." I reached out for her and she drew back.

"I know exactly what you meant," she said, and the room turned several degrees cooler. "That's not the first time I've heard that old Southern saying."

Her eyes were black pools of pain as she blinked back tears.

What a fool I was. I knew Santa Anna had raped her. She refused to discuss it. But since that first night, I'd learned she knew the passion of love, not just sex. Now I'd thrown out a careless thought, a foolish saying first uttered by young boys trying to brag about teen-age exploits.

She had been raped again. This time emotionally by someone she trusted, to whose bed she'd come willingly.

"Sweetness."

"I must not be too sweet for you to use those words."

Just like the moment before battle in New Orleans, I felt my stomach knot, then my bowels go so weak I was fearful I would lose them.

"Sweetness."

"General, you treat Indians better than my kind." She managed to sweep away the few tears that had formed.

"No. Not so." My throat tightened, my mouth went dry. I took a sip of coffee. "Give me a minute."

"Yessa masta. You jist tell this yellow girl what you want."

The words thundered in my ears. I closed my eyes, reaching into the depths of my quaking soul. This had to be made right. Letting out a long sigh, I began. "What I said was thoughtless."

She just stared at me. Her face an emotionless mask. I couldn't tell how she was hearing me. As a slave girl, as a lover, as a woman trying to understand the man she chose for a lover. A woman so utterly betrayed she'd maybe never find her way back to higher ground.

"The only defense I have is that I consider you an equal and said to you what I would flippantly have said to anyone."

The next few moments would define our relationship, forever.

"Emily …"

She held her hand up. "Stop. Before you go any further, General. I want to say something. Then, if you want to continue you can, or I can leave and we split the sheet."

I nodded. The tent was quiet. The fire snapped, flaring up just as my heart did. The happy aroma of coffee bubbling over the fire turned bitter in my nose. I wanted to hold her, bury my face in her dark hair, breath in her essence.

"Look here." She carefully pulled her peasant blouse over one shoulder, revealing a delicate yellow shoulder, then she held her hands up, turning them front to back, before lifting her skirt to her thighs. Dropping the skirt and pulling the blouse back over her shoulder, she approached me, bending to put her face so close I could feel its heat. Her breath, strangely alluring from coffee, wet my cheek. Then abruptly she pulled back.

"Did you see any black?"

A quick reply rose in my throat but I choked it back.

"Well, did you?" The words, barely about a whisper, held me as captive as any iron chain. My mind raced. Was there a correct answer? What did she want to hear? I was in command of nearly a thousand men yet this woman had reduced me to a stammering fool.

She cocked her head, waiting.

Finally a word fell from my lips, so soft I couldn't hear it myself, but my tongue had drawn it from the raw essence of my soul. Did she hear?

"Yellow."

I nodded.

"You didn't see black. You sure didn't see white, although my mother is mulatto because her mother was raped by her master, just as she was raped by her master and then I came along. Truth be known I've got about as much white blood in me as most of these Texicans running around seeking freedom. You just don't see it. How many half-white portions do you have to have to be considered pure enough to move past yellow? Milk. How much white milk does a nursing nigger have to give up to turn that pure plantation child black, or even yellow?"

She put her hand up when I started to reply. "Wait."

I swallowed, then took a sip of coffee.

"Have you ever wondered why a white man looks at someone like me and sees an African slave? They see the black, not the white. The mixture, the high yellow is not a good thing. We live in a nether world, the same world inhabited by haints and the spirits woodland gods, even if you've become a Christian and trust that God will someday do right by you."

She stopped, closed her eyes and seemed to withdraw into herself with a loud sigh.

"I made up my mind I wasn't going to bear any white man's child; maybe not have any children at all. It's too much a burden to bear, and then you compare me to coffee, black and strong."

She picked up the mugs holding the offending coffee and dumped what was left on the ground. Then she poured fresh, a slight tremor in her hand. She handed the mug to me.

"General, I give this to you not because it's black and strong, but because we shared something special last night, and you're the first man I've shared myself with that meant anything. The few others have been either meaningless or by force."

The hollers and clatters of an awakening camp drifted into the tent. She picked up her own cup ducked out the tent door into the waiting day.

CHAPTER TWENTY-FIVE

Message from the Alamo—March 14, 1836

I emerged from the tent to a scene of great activity. Calls and commands, clanking of metal, creaking of leather, whinnying of horses, and braying of mules. Women were already on their feet, hurrying into nearby bushes to attend to the day's first business before proceeding to whatever tasks they'd been assigned to get the expedition on the move.

The shrill voice of an angry man ordered, "Move your high yeller arse, girl. Even Houston's girl friend don't get to shirk around here."

Houston's girl friend? I was too amazed to get angry. Was that my reputation already? I had no time to brood, though, for I knew the urgency of crossing the Guadalupe and forging on to San Antonio. I looked forward to meeting Santa Anna again, this time with a whole army—such as it was—to back me up. I pictured him in irons. Why Toño. whatever happened to *mi amor?* It would be a delicious moment, and I would do whatever I could to help make it happen.

The first string of mules was halfway across the river when light sneaked through a break in the eastern clouds. The skies looked dark and ominous to the south and west, the very direction we were planning to travel. The wind was in our faces, flinging grit everywhere. After a cup of chicory and a mouthful of beans, having no assigned job and thinking where I might do the most good, I headed for the wagons. One man had borrowed himself a potful of grief trying to hitch up a four-mule team, so I took hold of lead animal's halter and sweet-talked him into calming down while the gentleman finished hooking up the harness.

"Don't know where you come from, gal, but you're sure welcome," he said. He stuck out his hand. "Name's Gil."

"Emily," I said. "I can drive this outfit if you got something better to do."

"I know you must be joking, Emily. It ain't woman's work. You're likely going to have to swim this across, and there's powder barrels in there. We can't afford to lose it."

"Take my word," I said. "I'm up to it."

"Then I know Jillian and my boy could use some help getting the rest of our goods loaded. General Houston's a great man, Emily, but what kind of war is this where you've got your whole family to take care of and worrying about fighting an army too?"

"Well, you worry about them, Gil. I've got this end taken care of." He thanked me and backed away, surveying the whole scene with a skeptical eye, as if he'd just turned over a bagful of treasure to a child for safekeeping. I waved. He finally waved back and trotted off.

These mules were no more cantankerous than dozens of others I'd handled first thing in the morning, so I moved them into line without a lot of trouble. The sight of me in the wagon seat with reins in my hands drew a lot of attention, most of it covert, though there were some pointed fingers and comments not to me directly, but loud enough to hear.

Houston rode back and forth through the camp, trying to keep things organized and purposeful. I fought down the idea that he was pretending to head up a real army. He was, after all, my only hope for getting out of this mess, and I needed to keep myself convinced he could do it.

It was near noon before my wagon neared the river and was on the brink of crossing over. As near as I could tell, everything had been going smoothly, if slowly. Despite the motely nature of our group, the operation proceeded with more efficiency and less rancor than Santa Anna's crossing. Maybe because these people had their own goods and families at stake, not to mention the idea of their own republic in their hearts.

Then came the sound of shouting and the sight of a racing pony on the far side of the river, and everything stopped.

The shout was for Houston, and the pony carried Deef Smith, whom Houston had sent out the previous day to scout for hostiles along our route to San Antonio. Apparently, I figured, he'd found some. But his news turned out to be far worse than that.

****

Houston galloped up to meet him, and he and Deef stood off to the side a hundred yards or so, conferring. Houston's head was down, his eyes on the ground. Deef was gesticulating madly. While they talked, another group approached at a much slower space. A couple of women were riding double while a man led their horse. Others straggled behind.

After a while, Houston mounted up and head back toward us. Smith was by his side, furiously objecting to something. Finally, Houston had had enough and put up his hand, and Smith shut up. When he got close enough, the general called. "General Council. Right over there." He pointed to a small rise with a scooped out hilltop near some willows. "Fast as ever you can get here."

I hitched my mules to a Palo Verde and eased over toward where the meeting was to take place. I found myself beside Gil and Jillian moving in the same direction.

"What's this council?"

"General's got us divided up into groups of a hundred. Each group chose a leader. That's the council."

I just nodded. It wasn't long before fifty or so men had gathered around Houston, and he sat them down, but stood up himself. I gathered the council was supposed to be more or less private, but that didn't stop the rest of us from crowding as close as we could to hear whatever transpired.

When he'd got everyone sat down, Houston called, "Hardy, would you bring them on in here, please."

Presently, the women we'd seen across the river entered the circle, the hems of their dresses still wet from swimming the horse across the river.

"This is Mrs. Susan Dickinson and Mrs. Betsy Tolliver," Houston said. "They have a message for all of us."

The two women looked at one another, and finally, Mrs. Dickinson, her face covered with grime and her lank hair falling out of her bonnet, shook her head and said something to the general I couldn't hear. He nodded and took a breath.

"These ladies say they can't talk about this any more, so it's up to me to speak. I'll put it plain as I can. The Alamo has fallen."

Of course there was an uproar and a volley of curses and cries to go after Santa Anna and get revenge. But that was nothing compared to what happened after Houston's next bombshell.

"Mrs. Dickinson and Mrs. Tolliver have been through a great trial. They were captured by the Mexicans, then released on their own to wander through hostile territory and die. It was only Providence that led Deef Smith and Mr. Hardy here to them in time to bring them here to safety."

Houston held up his hand and let the cries die down before he continued. "Given what's happened and the information we now have about Santa Anna's movements, I know what our strategy must be."

Another outcry. Another raised hand from Houston. "I know you all want to avenge ourselves against that so-called Napoleon imitator, and no one wants that more than I do. But we have to let strategy overcome our emotions. And strategy at this point dictates that we turn back."

Every man in the council leaped to his feet, waving fists and shouting.

Some of them leaped on to their horses and galloped toward the river, waving muskets. A few of them actually fired in the air. I feared my general had lost control of his army entirely and that there was no hope of defeating Santa Anna or anyone and that the entire republic was lost.

There was no hope of being heard over the hullabaloo, so Houston decided on action instead. He mounted up and headed toward the wagons. The wagon ahead of mine had been just about to enter the current. The mules' feet were in six inches of swampy water, and the driver had tied them to a cypress stump sticking above the water. Houston dismounted, unhitched them, remounted, and turned team and wagon a hundred and eighty degrees till they headed eastward. Eager for a chance to help, I ran to my own team and hopped onto the wagon seat.

"Haw," I yelled, giving the whip a pop, more for show than because I needed it. "Move on you devils." And soon it was Houston's wagon and mine with their backs to the Guadalupe.

It was a while before others started to follow suit, but eventually, the entire outfit had reversed direction. Houston hurried back across the river to coordinate the recrossing of all who had spent most of the morning getting themselves from the east to the west bank. The mood ranged from angry to glum. It had been the thought of saving the Alamo that had brought this group all the way across the plains and over two great rivers, and now it was lost and instead of forging out to meet the enemy we were turning tail.

And then came probably the biggest surprise of the whole campaign, and it came from a twelve-year-old boy. I'd been gathering wool, somber as anyone, when Zachary suddenly turned up seated beside me.

"Miss Emily, everyone's so discouraged. Don't we still have a chance against those pepperbellies?"

"Of course we still have a chance. It's just kind of setback is all, and it's got everyone down in the dumps."

"Well, seems to me like we can't allow that, Miss Emily."

I smiled. "Oh, we can't?"

"No miss Emily. We've got to keep a stiff upper lip and go after it ever' minute till we revenge all them brave men what died at the Alamo. We can't never forget them."

"I don't think anyone ever will, Zach."

"Then why don't we act like it?"

"You tell 'em, Zach," I said. I said it more to indulge him than anything else, without any notion of what effect my words might have. The next thing I knew, Zach had jumped down from my wagon and started running down the line, shouting for all he was worth.

"Perk up, everyone. We got to remember the Alamo. Remember the Alamo."

He hadn't gone too far down the line till other folks took up the cry, and "Remember the Alamo," sounded up and down the line and across the plains. And so was born the motto that was to carry us through all the way to San Jacinto and beyond.

CHAPTER TWENTY-SIX

Colorado Surprises

Zach's battle cry was invigorating all right, but it was thin gruel for our company in the face of our other difficulties. The rain. The cold. The mud. The skimpy rations. The rancor of the men who wanted to ride after Santa Anna despite Houston's admonitions to keep moving east. Keep moving, that is to say, back in the direction they'd already traversed. Keep, that is to say, retreating.

Plenty of men supported the General, telling the malcontents that if they felt up to playing general they might want study up under Andy Jackson the way Houston had at New Orleans. That shut them up for a while, but it's my experience with such as them their main activity is above all to protest. Jesus Christ himself couldn't have produced enough loaves and fishes to satisfy their hunger for complaining. Before long they were right back at it, saying we should circle up, build some breastworks and wait for the Mexicans who were surely on our heels. Houston stayed solid, though, and kept repeating that they'd get all the action they wanted when the time was right. But not yet. We lost some men to that argument, but we gained a few, too. Our numbers went up and down, it seemed, by the hour, and you would have needed a Chinaman speedy with an abacus to keep track.

It wasn't till the third day out from Gonzales, fetching water for my mules from a small creek that I met someone who was going to affect my life almost as much as Houston himself. I'd just filled a second bucket, picked up my first, and turned to go when I nearly collided with the first dark-skinned person I'd seen since leaving Morgan's Point. I managed not to drop my buckets, but felt frozen to the spot, as was he.

"I … " I said. Then shook my head.

"What … " he answered, just as eloquently.

Then we both laughed. I put down my burden and stepped aside so others could get to the water.

"Joe," he said, extending a hand.

"Emily." We clasped hands briefly. "Where in the world did you come from?"

"The Alamo."

"Do tell. I'd like to hear that story."

"I done told it to others, but no one could understand it like one of us."

"True enough. My wagon's close by. Maybe we could ride a ways?"

"You got a team and a wagon?" He cocked his head, furrowed his forehead. I laughed at his astonishment. "For right now. So join me?"

"Soon's I deliver my water. I ain't attached to no one in particular. For right now, that is. Seems like we both got stories to tell."

We attracted a lot of attention, did Joe and I that day, especially from those on foot as we sat side by side up on the wagon seat. Some of the looks we got were curious, others pure poison. We both knew we couldn't continue in this vein for long, but neither could we let go of the kindred moment.

"Colonel Travis was my master, and he was a good one, if you gots to have a master."

"And now you have none, Joe," I said. "You could just run north."

"Don't think I didn't consider it, don't consider it every day, in fact. But in some ways it's more dangerous out there than here. Indians don't much care what kind of hair's on top of a scalp. Plus I'm what the slavers consider prime goods—young and in good shape. Who knows who they'd sell me back to?"

I nodded, thinking of my own trek across the desert. Even though Joe was a man, there were perils aplenty.

"And there's another thing." A moment of silence followed. I let it stand till Joe was ready to go on. He shook his head. "I got a feeling during that battle, Emily. Travis told me to pick up a gun. No master ever wants a gun in the hand of his slave. I know he meant me to shoot at them Mexicans, and it never probably crossed his mind, but it did mine." Another silence. I was about to ask him what it was crossed his mind, but I realized I knew already. "I could have just as well have fired on him and all of a sudden have been a free man. Even if them pepperbellies wiped us it out and it was only for a little while, I'd have died free."

"Why didn't you do it?" I said. "I think I might have."

"I don't know. But I started firing on them red uniforms instead, right along with all the white men and the few others of our kind that was stuck behind them 'dobe walls, and people kept getting shot, and then Master Travis himself took one through the head, and then the whole place was full of Mexicans running over the bodies like they was no more than stepping stones, and by that time, I was feeling more like a Texican than a slave."

"And do you still?" I said.

"At first, the feeling was strong in me. After Mexicans made sure all the white folks was dead, they called out for Negroes—"Nay-grows," in that strange way they have that made it hard for us to figure out what they was saying for a time. A few of us stepped out, thinking maybe we might be saved. We all knew the law said slavery was outlawed in Mexico, though we knew also that the law was something many didn't abide by. Turned out they wasn't after slaves, but after killing us same as they had the Texicans. Those of us who escaped their knives and guns was lucky we did. Right then I was ready to fight for the republic or die. Now, I goes back and forth. Sometimes I think I'm part of General Houston's army, other times I feels like I'm just hiding out and some slave-hunter's going to come along and deliver me back into perdition."

"Joe." I said. "What's your last name?"

"Travis, I guess. Like my master. Never knowed no other."

"I'm lucky enough to be Emily West, though I don't know my daddy. He freed my mother, then disappeared." I told him my story, then, how I'd been hired as a free woman, then how Santa Anna treated me, burned my papers and all. Afterwards, it was my turn to be silent. Joe respected that for some time. When he finally spoke, it was a truth that no white person—not even the General, could truly understand.

"So, without them papers, you no better off than me. Far as the law's concerned, we both fugitive slaves no matter what other good works we might have done. And from what I overhear," Joe went on, "there's them that want this new Republic to be no better than Mississippi and them."

"Let's hope not, Joe," I said. "Let's hope not."

***

Joe and I rode together throughout the day, he taking the reins sometimes to relieve me. He was right that we were two of a kind, and I felt a strong bond of friendship with him. Through the day, as we rode, I searched my heart for signs of affection beyond friendship, but nothing stirred. Well, that's not quite true, but what stirred was an affection for something unattainable, and I put it aside and quit searching.

By twilight, we knew we'd used up all the extended time together we could afford. The hostility toward my having a wagon to myself and my supposed favored position with the General had caused agitation enough. Add Joe to the mix, and we were liable to start a conflagration we couldn't control. However, I convinced him to prolong our ride until Houston called for the company to bed down for the night. Then circumstances took matters out of our hands.

***

We'd almost returned to the Colorado. Even though it was considerably upstream from where Colleen had gone under, it still gave me the willy's to think of coming near it again. The right rear wheel of my wagon dropped into a bog, and the team couldn't move the load. Joe leaped down and tried to turn it by hand, but couldn't by himself. A couple of other men soon joined him. There was no feeling of color or station at moments like this, and everyone worked together. My eyes traveled back and forth between the wheel and my team, and on one such transition, I saw the women approaching out of the southern gloom.

"Look there," I yelled, pointing with the whip I'd been using to lash the mules. "Off to the right."

It wasn't unusual to see stragglers wandering toward the convoy. But unaccompanied women, just two of them, made for a unique combination. Most often, we'd see a family, or maybe a woman and a child or two where Apaches had killed the man and somehow missed the rest of the family.

I jumped down from the wagon and started toward them. The men left the wagon wheel and followed. The closer I got, the more sure I was who one of the women was. There was no mistaking those broad shoulders and the blocky form which had taken up so much space in the coaches where we'd ridden side by side.

"Kitty Jo," I yelled. "That you? Really you?"

"Emily?" came the cry back. "Don't tell me."

We ran toward one another, or as close to running as the sloppy earth would allow, and fell into one another's arms.

"Lordy," she said. "I never featured this at all. Never in a thousand."

For the moment, I forgot about my wagon and even Joe and didn't care at all whether I got back across the river. Not that Kitty Jo and I had ever been so very close, but one of the few pleasant memories of the Santa Anna times was the sisterhood among us Morgan's Point women. Colleen and I both had felt bad about leaving them behind, and their fates had crossed my mind often even amid my own troubles.

"This here's Mary Rose, Emily," Kitty said. "I done found her lying in the bushes right near where the Indians burned her cabin flat to the ground and her husband and children along with it."

Indeed, Mary Rose looked like someone more beast than human. Her eyes were glazed over, and she kept wringing her hands and shaking her head like she was denying something every minute. She didn't acknowledge me at all, and Kitty Jo shrugged her shoulders. There was little flesh on Kitty Jo's frame, and Mary Rose had gone even longer without food than she had.

I turned to ask Joe to fetch the general post haste, but he had disappeared, so I asked the nearest man. Then I helped the women inside my wagon, where I pulled a couple of blankets from out of the other freight and assisted them in getting out of their wet clothes. We were in the middle of that when the general's voice boomed from outside.

"Emily, what's so damned important?"

I left Kitty Jo to finish swaddling Emily Rose and made my way back to the wagon seat.

"Hello, General," I said. "Haven't seen you in a couple of days."

"Been busy, Emily. Still am. You didn't bring me back here just to pass the time of day?"

"No sir," I said. "You know I wouldn't be so presumptuous. Or you would know if you'd taken the time for a simple conversation or two." I hadn't planned to get so snippy with him, but it just came out like that, and I didn't feel like taking it back, either. "There's someone here I think you should meet."

"All right, let's meet him, then, so we can get on with this war."

"It's not a him. It's a her. And I think once you talk to her you might find she'll be a big help in getting on with this war."

"Then let's talk," he said.

"She's had a long walk, and she's soaked, but I think a warm fire and a meal would bring her up to sharing at least a word or two.

"I can't just—"

"She came straight here from Santa Anna's camp," I said.

That stopped him. "Well, we've only got couple of hours travel time left today anyhow," he said. And he rode off, ordering everyone to camp for the night.

***

Kitty Jo and Mary Rose were still wrapped in their blankets, sitting beside a meager fire, though neither was any longer unclothed beneath. I'd managed to borrow a shift and a nightgown for them to use while their own garments dried. It was barely dark, and though they'd consumed a few beans, they'd had no time to rest. But Houston was impatient to get on with his interview. Concerned though I was for my companions, I didn't blame the General for his hunger after information.

"Santa Anna," he said. "What's happening there?"

"I don't know too much," Kitty Jo said. "I wasn't privileged like her nibs, here. Sorry, Emily. That came out meaner than I meant it."

I just nodded.

"What about you?" That question was directed to Mary Rose, who had refused to leave Kitty Jo's side, clung to her like a toddler to her mother. She raised her head at the question, but appeared to look at Houston without really seeing him. Kitty Jo patted her hand.

"It's no use, General. She was never was with us and the Mexicans, and she's been through a horror that's set her askew."

Houston didn't ask for details. "All right. You then. You may not know much, but you know something. Out with it."

As it turned out, Kitty had been traveling afoot for close on to a week, just heading in the general direction of northeast, hoping to bump into us. Her wandering had been near as hellish as mine, except she'd had no Chief Bowl to rescue her along the way. After Colleen and I had escaped, the Mexicans had dragged her and the other Morgan's Point women all the way to San Antonio, where she'd been chained together while the soldiers went into battle against the brave defenders of the Alamo.

I could see the pain pass like a summer storm across Houston's face as she spoke. From what he'd told me earlier, I knew he was recalling with anger how James Bowie had disobeyed his orders to demolish the place and get out. The slaughter had been unnecessary, and the cause of the new republic had lost some valuable warriors for no good reason. That was the military price. In the matter of his heart, many of those men had held a high place in his affections. He'd miss them forever. But all that had no place in the present discussion.

"And after the Alamo?" he said.

"I'm not sure," Kitty Jo said. "It seemed like maybe the Mexicans thought they'd won everything. I'd been parceled out to a captain who got killed on the second day. They didn't get around to blessing me with a new partner till two days after the massacre, and then to a lieutenant so young I guess he didn't know his musket from his gun, if you get my meaning. Could be he's still trying to figure which is which 'cause he never got around to me the whole three days we were supposed to be together. I just slipped into the bushes one morning to do my business and walked away."

"Good for you," I said. But Houston was not in the mood for small talk and congratulations.

"You said they thought they'd won everything. What did they do?"

"Well, General, they started talking about you. My lieutenant's English wasn't much shucks, but he kept saying, "We kill Houston now, we kill Tehan woman." What you think now, Tehan woman?"

"And the army?"

"I don't know. I wish I did. But from what little I could see. It seemed to me like things were kind of disorganized after that. There wasn't so much spit and polish as before. Lots more yelling, and big bunches of men riding and marching off in different directions. And a lot more tents around the edges of the army."

"Some for protection, some for what you might call moonlight commerce is my guess," Houston said.

"I have a question for you, General," Kitty Jo, said. "Who's Flores?"

"What about him?"

"That was another name besides yours my little lieutenant mentioned. First Flores, then Houston."

It was the first time I'd seen Houston smile since he'd approached my wagon that afternoon. It wasn't all that much of a smile, but it did pierce the gloom some. "Salvador Flores. He was supposed to be running a rear guard action along with a few pickup troops after we left Gonzales. I haven't heard a thing from him. Afraid he'd been wiped out, but sounds like he's still fighting. This is the best news you've told me so far, Kitty Jo."

But Kitty Jo hadn't even been able to wait for the answer to her question. Her chin was on her chest, her big shoulders drooping. Mary Rose had long ago laid her head on one of those shoulders.

"These two are more than exhausted, General."

"Indeed, Emily. What you said about how valuable their information might be? More than true. Santa Anna hates the distractions of all those camp followers. It'll mean he thinks his discipline is unraveling. And big bunches of men hurrying off in various directions may mean he's splitting up his army because he's not sure where's best to attack. We'll soon have him where we want him."

"Wonderful, General. We all can use a lift. Now let me get my friends to the women's tent."

"Once that's done, Emily, you think you can find your way back here?"

So there it was again. At last.

"You sure you want to risk it again?" I asked.

"Well, I am the general," he answered. "What about you?"

Even after after our emotional reunion at Gonzales, I'd seen little of Houston, and I'd about decided I'd be lucky to get my savings back, let alone build more between us, despite the fact that other women had me tagged as his favorite. I smiled.

"Well then," he said.

I smiled and walked over to Kitty Jo. "Come on, dear. Time you got yourself a good dry rest."

I glanced back over my shoulder. Sam was still smiling.

"Good night, General," I said. And I winked. He winked back. Gestures worth a thousand words. At least.

CHAPTER TWENTY-SEVEN

Bounty Hunters— March 20, 1836

Sometimes you just don't like the looks of a situation. Sometimes the players make Shylock look like the court jester.

Sometimes the players wear a look that betrays their villainy. The three men sat easy, obviously used to calling the shots. We'd had a bit of snow, and I know early April can be a little chilly, but all three had on long, dark dusters that were out of place in the warming temperature. They looked like the cook had stamped them all out with the same cookie cutter that morning. Pistols tied to their thighs, worn gloves, checkered flour-sack shirts peeked out from the wrist of their dusters and under leather vests, and dusty gray Stetsons shaded faces accented by handle-bar mustaches. Manacles hung from saddle horns.

No trouble spotting their mission.

I looked at Erastus, he nodded and grinned. I know both of us were thinking that their Momma was back at the campsite, otherwise how would they get dressed?

"Howdy, General. These here's my brothers, Zeke and Ike. They call me Cain."

"We come for the nigger slave, Joe. The one that belonged to Will

Travis," said the one on the far right, squinting slightly into the sun behind my back.

"First of all that's Lieutenant Colonel Travis, a bona fide hero in these parts and soon around the world I suspect."

"We knowed Will since he was a whippersnapper. Not surprised his uppity ways got him killed," he said, slowly drawing the glove off his right hand. Erastus saw it and moved further to my right to set up crossfire.

Up until then I was ready to give him Travis's slave. He didn't mean anything to me. The slavery issue was becoming as big an issue in Texas as it was at the founding of the United States. No telling how it would turn out for our new Republic, but no one was going to disrespect a brave man who died for freedom.

"I told you, Colonel—I emphasized the word, hitting each syllable—Travis is a respected patriot. Show respect."

Gloves came off the hands of the other riders and I saw Erastus ease his pistol out of its holster. I nodded and my Texicans quickly surrounded the trio, taking the bit of each horse in hand.

"Now, if you want to ask nice. I might give you an answer."

"Hell," Erastus' sotto voice made them frown. "We'd even give ya shot and food to join us in avenging Colonel Travis' death and all those at the Alamo."

"What about it, gentlemen? Care to join us?"

Their leader looked me in the eyes. There was no escaping the situation. He looked away, then carefully, hand held high, reached into the vest pocket.

"This here paper gives us the right to claim that boy and take him back to the Travis family."

"You boys bounty hunters?"

"We got the right to take that nigger back with us."

"I'll tell you what. Joe was shot at and damned near killed while defending the Alamo. He even killed some Mexicans. He may be black, but he's still a hero to us. But we don't want to break your law. Give 'im a few more days to get back on his feet and he's yours."

I addressed the gathering crowd. "Boys give these fellers a taste of Texas hospitality. Tell Miz Emmy the first round is on me. "Course this tent ain't much of a bar, but the rot-gut is first class. You're welcome to it, such as it is."

Erastus made his way to me as the men shoved into the tent-saloon.

"She heard everything. She's peeking around the flap."

I whispered to Deef, "Time Joe headed North, to the promised land. It sure isn't here."

I raised my voice. "You hear me in there, Emily?"

Emily called, "Loud and clear, General. Belly up to the bar, boys. Drinks on the house."

CHAPTER TWENTY-EIGHT

In the General's Tent

Emily reached across to take my hand. I cradled it in mine. It was calloused, yet amazingly soft for a woman who spent her life working. A sturdy hand that washed clothes, chopped wood, hoed a garden and kept meticulous bar books, yet still another one of those inconsistencies that wrap this woman in a conundrum. Like her heritage, not black, not white, but "high yeller", neither one nor the other.

"Joe said Bowie died on a stretcher surrounded by dead Mexican soldiers," she said softly, gently tugging to retrieve her hand. I wouldn't let it go. "He said they were stacked like some much cord wood around his bed. One even lay on top of him, gutted."

"Did he bring the knife?"

She shook her head. "No. I asked, too. He didn't see it."

"Some lowlife is flashing it around, bragging about taking it from Bowie," I said, the injustice of such an ignoble death flushing my spine. My mind rejected the thought. Maybe it wasn't ignoble. He died fighting for a cause, for his family, in his city, dedicated to freedom. My mind trembled at the concept of dying in such a blaze of glory. When it came my time, perhaps a just God would grant me that special moment.

Yet, I didn't admit that. "It was a noble death. It compares to the

Spartans at Thermopylae, fighting to the last sword thrust. These men in the Alamo, and at Goliad, will be avenged."

"Your best vengeance will be to lead the Texicans to victory, to establish a great nation of freedom, under God's rule," she said.

"I've always recognized a Higher Being," I said. "Hell, I even got baptized a Catholic just so I could become a Texican. But that slaughter in San Antonio, so many good men dead, makes me wonder just whose side He is on."

"He'll always be on your side, General Houston, because your side is righteous."

"Call me Sam."

I looked at her, the fire bouncing off her dark curly hair and tawny skin. Her eyes were black pools absorbing the flames, bubbling with streaks of red and orange and yellow. Tears of compassion rolled down her cheeks.

"Define righteous," I asked.

"It'd be easy to say all the things preachers say, the ones found in the good book like don't steal, don't kill, and don't lie. But your righteous comes from your heart. Righteous to you is freedom. A man's right to determine his own destiny."

I tightened my grip when she tugged again.

"You know you're hurting me."

"Then don't pull back."

"That's what white men have told me all my life. Don't pull back."

The silence was pregnant with her hidden meaning. Was I as guilty as all the others? The rapists, the abusers, the ones who ordered her about? I loosened my grip and she retrieved her hand. She hesitated for a moment, grinned shyly, then put it back onto my open palm.

"You don't have…"

"I know," she said, placing a finger on my lips.

"May I?"

"I've never been asked before."

I put her hand back on her lap, took her face in both hands and drew her to me. She came willingly.

CHAPTER TWENTY-NINE

Making Heroes

Big Foot Wallace's moccasins slipped out of sight in the black muddy clay as he bellowed cadence. He pulled up one foot now sporting only a dripping wool sock, and bent to search under the grime for the missing moccasin.

"Hut, two, three four." He didn't miss a beat, standing there moccasin in hand, mud to his ankles as light rain and a sprinkling of snow settled on his red beard. His responsibility charged right by him, each foot slapping mud. With a shrug, he jammed his big foot back into the muddy mess, yanked a thong free of his fringed coat, tied the moccasin in place as a young frontiersman dropped out of formation to offer help.

His offer was met with a shove. "Get back in line, boy. We ain't done drillin' yet. Ya gotta learn discipline." The confused youth struggled to regain his place.

A giggle told me she was behind me. I didn't acknowledge her.

"After your Pa lost his leg I done told him I was bringing you back for summer harvest and you ain't gonna make it less'n you learn to follow orders," Big foot called after the running boy.

It was a sorry mess. Big Foot had his ragtag group marching before we pulled up camp and started on toward the Louisiana border. What was left of the regular army was shooting at targets under Mailbu Lamar's supervision. Another small group mended tents and reins and wagon wheels and single trees and thousands of other details; nothing was thrown away. Across the way men formed lines for their morning gruel. At least it was hot.

Stragglers surrounded my army, all camping as close as possible with the hope of some protection. Actually the troops were blessed by this because most of those seeking safety shared what hot breakfast they had and it was a welcome addition to the gruel. Most of the men failed to bring the "required" three day's rations with them—originally the requirement had been ten days' supplies—I shrugged mentally. We were long past that.

"General." Her voice came softly, a sweet distraction to duty. I still hesitated until I smelled the sharp coffee I assumed she held out. When I turned, she appeared astride a tiny pony. She held the coffee in one hand, and with the other she offered a basket of cornbread fresh off the griddle. A feast under these circumstances.

Her arms were bare, prickled with cold. Only a light scarf tried to ward off the cold. Her warm breath puffed around her face. I reached behind me and took out my sleeping blanket. Spurring my mount forward, wrapped it around her shoulders, dropping the ends gentle over her breasts.

"No, General."

"You can give it back to me tonight when we make camp."

"But some will know it's your blanket."

I fixed her gaze. "So?"

I was rewarded with another blush that surprised me. I knew she was a woman of the world, probably through no fault of her own.

She lowered her head, then raised it, tears tugging at the corners of her eyes. "Thank you."

"If you don't drink the coffee. Right now. It's going to be colder than a witch's heart," she said, shaking it slightly for emphasis. "And I have more."

Glancing back at the tableau, I still hesitated.

"General, even though they're hungry themselves, they would want you to take nourishment. The leader needs to be strong."

"And you, who supplies the leader, have you eaten?"

"I sneaked some while riding over here."

I took the basket, lifted out a small slice, then returned it to her and took the coffee. The mug was still hot when I lifted it to my lips for a sip. Steam awakened feelings in my chilled nostrils. Then I took a bite of the cornbread, which was now cold. Another sip of coffee melted the coarse mixture and it eased down my throat with a hint of sweetness.

"You make it?"

She nodded. "You eat another," I said. "Sometimes I think these men need you—especially your spying skills—more than they need me."

Her light skin darkened at the compliment.

"Like Moses, you are leading them to the promised land, although they already stand on it," she said.

"Maybe it's Armageddon,"

"If it is, then they have their God-given leader. They will win."

I nodded "If angels sit on their shoulders they surely will. After all, the patriarch Abraham entertained angels unawares."

"General."

I looked down to see our brave boy Zachary standing at attention.

"I have a message from my colonel," he said, offering a crisp piece of parchment with a dirty hand that rivaled the mud on his face. His eyes darted to the cornbread, then whipped back to attention.

"Thank you, son." He started to leave, mud sucking at his shoes.

I said, "Good to see you again, Zach. I bet you'd like a bit of cornbread for breakfast."

"Yes, sir."

Instead of offering him a piece of cornbread, Sweetness handed Zach the whole basket. He looked at me and I nodded.

"You have any more of that coffee, Miss Emily?"

"I do," she said as Zach fumbled for the tin cup tied to his belt.

She poured it full. She ruffled his hair, then took her scarf off to tie it around his head, securing his ears. "Best to go somewhere private, eat slowly and don't gulp it down."

"No Ma'am."

As he trudged off, Emily began to chuckle softly until she could contain her mirth any longer and her laughter rang out. "Talk about entertaining angels unaware."

She split the last of the coffee, handed me a cup.

"Just as I like it," I said. "Hot and sweet."

We traded a look that said we had mended our fences. Or were at least on the way. She almost smiled, in fact. We huddled under my blanket while I read the dispatch.

Mexican scouts had been seen on the other side of the Colorado. A chill seized me, colder than the icy grip that had become my constant companion.

"Hey, Zach." He turned to snap to attention, nearly spilling his coffee. "Does anyone else know what's in this dispatch?"

"No, sir…well…maybe…"

"Who, boy? I need to know."

"Well Mr. Smith gave it to my Pa to bring. It kinda fell open and he saw it so he sent me on with it. He's gathering a group to go whip them Pepperbellies." He nodded enthusiastically. "Even said I might could go."

He paused, almost shy. "He said I could go even after big brother Ryan died at the Alamo."

"And your Pa's name?"

"Schott."

I dismissed him with a wave. That's all I needed. A rowdy bunch, likely drunk, fighting under their own initiative stumbling around in the woods in the dark, shooting each other up and giving away our location. Thanks to the generosity of the Groce family, we'd had a good week at their plantation. The men had drilled, had a little hot food, and discovered a little discipline. At least as much as a hard-headed

Texican could bow to.

True to his Germanic ancestry, Schott had taken to the discipline and even had the men from his home town of Medina high-stepping it through the mud.

But we weren't ready to fight. I shook my head when Sweetness handed me the coffee and she thought I was rejecting it. She started to pull back and I grasped it. She let go.

"Trying to lead this army I like herding frogs," I said. "Everyone has an opinion and goes their own way. The dispatch says a scouting party of maybe thirty soldados is right over there beyond that grove." I pointed across the meadow at a thick stand of live oak trees. "They probably can hear the gunfire as we practice, maybe even the sucking sounds of boots in mud. Deef wants to know what I want to do. He wants to attack and send those devils to purgatory. Nobody seems to understand the concept of a strategic retreat. There's plenty of time for blood to run hot."

I hung back. This hadn't been my plan. It was Schott, not me, who was the leader of this group. I had borrowed a horse, found a coonskin hat, and thrown a dark cloak over myself. No one was going to locate the General in this garb.

As we rode to engage the heathen, energy flashed from man to man, a lightning bolt welding each mind to a common goal. These were not professional soldiers but ordinary civilians, although you call a Texican ordinary, you're hankering for trouble. A blacksmith, several youth too fresh to shave, farmers, butchers, bakers, even a candlestick maker, a store clerk rode with his apron flapping. Schott had gathered most of the able-bodied men from Medina, all hell-bent on protecting home and hearth and family.

Mounted on the family's prized plough horse, a Percheron some nineteen hands high, Zach towered above the other combatants. I slowed down to match his pace at the rear of the charge.

As we swarmed into the camp I realized this was the first time I'd seen any of my army in combat. They weren't like the finally honed troops lead by Ol' Hickory. Each man spurred his horse forward, spitting epithets questioning the virtue of all the mothers of the enemy, along with their choice of food. It might have been comical except men were dying on both sides of the line in the full-throated roar of voice and rifle fire.

To my right, one thin voice pierced the thunder of war. "Remember the Alamo. Remember the …" It gurgled to a stop. I turned to see Zach splayed backwards. With no hand on the reins, the horse now stood, head down, sides heaving, blood trickling down its withers. I grabbed the reins, hoping to lead Zach to safety in a tight grove of aspen trees.

Musket balls slammed into the side of the Percheron and he stumbled, falling forward on his knees. Zach lay glassy-eyes his lips barely moving as the Twenty-Third Psalm hissed through bloody lips.

"You're going to be okay," I said, taking his hands. We both knew it was a lie but it was the best I could do. In a whisper, I joined him in uttering his last words, ones of hope. When we finished, he grabbed my arm, pending death giving him a strength he didn't have in life.

"General, that's you ain't it?"

I took off the coonskin hat so he could see me clearly. "Yes, Zach, it's me."

The revelation put him in awe. "I actually got to fight the heathen right alongside you, General. Wait'll my Pa finds out."

Pain roiled his body. "I can see my brother waiting there for me. I know it's him because his front tooth's missing and he's got red hair."

Zach coughed and more blood spilled out his mouth and down his chin,

"You're gonna beat those Pepperbellies, General. Promise me."

"Yes we are."

"My brother's pretty impressed that I know the General, but I gotta go with him. Tell Ma I love her, and that I seed my brother."

I nodded, and he closed his eyes, then they snapped open, fully awake, comprehending, pulling me closer to his face. A spray of blood settled on my forehead and cheeks.

"When you whip up on 'em, tell our boys to remember the Alamo, and all the boys I'm going to join."

Then, as men have died through the ages, he was gone. His eyes lost their luster and his grip relaxed.

I used my pistol to put the slobbering horse out of its misery as whooping irregulars begin to surround me, the joy of victory fading into reality.

"That's Schott's boy." The voice came from behind me.

"Someone had better go get him."

Caught unprepared, most of the enemy had stripped to long johns and tucked into bedrolls so it was a short battle, over by the time Zach had died. We lost some good men, but the enemy was routed.

Schott walked up to his son, gasping for air, fighting the heaving sobs that choked his breathing.

"I only got one boy left."

"Then he'd best stay home with his Ma, until this is over."

"I didn't think …"

"None of you thought," I said, sweeping my arms to encompass the circle of men. "None of you thought. You were all spoiling for a fight. I was retreating to set a trap for Santa Anna, and we can still set that trap. But you need to follow orders."

I knew it sounded harsh, especially to a freshly grieving father.

"Don't let Zach's death be in vain, or any of the other men who died today. The next time we'll be ready and we will win.

"Now, take this boy home to his Ma."

CHAPTER THIRTY

The return of Cain And his brothers

Zeke. Ike. Cain. Who in their right mind would name a child after the original murderer? Chunky, bearded and shifty-eyed, he looked the part. Either this trio's parents rutted like rabbits or their mother spent hours reading the good book.

Whatever the case, the result was regrettable to say the least. The thought of what it took to bring this trio into the world was beyond my ken. Cain, if he had his way, was going to get all my men killed.

"I say we attack and we do it now. Right now," Cain said, thumping a ham-fisted hand on the plank across two barrels that served as a bar. Emily jumped and straightened the sheet that draped the plank.

"Well, after we finish our beer," Zeke chimed in.

"Damn straight," Ike said on cue.

The problem was they were riling up some good men. The one we called Mountain Man was spoiling for a fight. He was big and a strange combination of ferocious and compassionate. Right now he looked the former, a man to inspire fear. The bounty hunters suddenly lost their menacing look. Towering more than six feet, his tomahawk tucked in his belt, it was easy to see how the frontiersman had earned his nickname.

No one knew his Christian name. For all we knew it might be on the wall in a sheriff's office. He had followed old Ben Milam in the original battle of San Antonio. That had gone well at first. They'd driven the Mexicans out of San Antonio, though the damned chilipeppers had later regrouped and marched back on the city.

"I think we should give this a bit more thought." Juan Seguin could have died at the Alamo, but Travis had sent him for recruits. By the time he gathered a few at Gonzales, the citadel had fallen. I couldn't tell if he wished to have been a part of that senseless sacrifice or happy to survive to fight another day.

As he emptied his mug, Cain's bloodshot eyes flashed evil through the beer that had loosened his tongue.

"What you got to say about it, Mescan? You took off from the Alamo soon as Santa Anna's troops showed up."

Juan's slender frame stiffened as Deef's hand shot out in restraint. It was enough to distract Juan before he shook the hand free of his shoulder.

"Juan," Deef said softly, a deadly thread in his usually friendly voice. "He ain't worth it. Ifen he was, I'd be the first across the floor."

Juan turned to look over Deef's shoulder at me. I gave him a barely perceptible shake of the head. We needed aggressiveness, but we also needed unity.

"Tell you what . . . what's your name again?" I cocked my head in mock forgetfulness.

"Cain."

"That's right . . . Cain. Where's your mark? Didn't God give you one like the first murderer?"

His eyes bulged, his jaw trembled, and his hand fell to the butt of the pistol stuffed in his belt. His brothers put down their beers and sidled next to him, their hands sliding to the ready, about as subtle as a whore's come hither.

In return, Deef's hand rested on his pistol, the other on Juan's shoulder. Mountain Man leaned back on the bar his hand inches from his tomahawk.

The late April chill swept across the outdoor bar. You could hear horses slushing in the mud, men cursing their fate and somewhere in the distance a mockingbird.

One wrong word and this loose-knit band of brothers would turn into blazing enemies. I really wanted to challenge their mother's virtue, an insult even this scum could not ignore. But in reality, I needed every man's son that I could assemble to defeat Santa Anna. So, I had to control my boiling blood and tame my tongue. Not an easy task as the hairs prickled across my neck, the first sign my body was ready for battle. I forced it to relax.

"Some folks think Juan, here, has a mark."

Juan cut his eyes at me, questioning. Deef held tighter, even placing his hand over Juan's.

On the other side of the bar I saw Emily nod as her hands went out of sight behind the sheet on the bar. I knew they rested on a scatter gun that could take out all three with one blast.

"You think he might bear a mark, even without him realizing it because his skin's a bit different. What we have here is a distinct group of men called Texicans. Most were born under the heavy yoke of Mexican dictatorship. Even Juan, here, knows that yoke. But of white or Mexican descent, anyone born on this sacred land is a Texican, part Texan, part Mexican, but all Texican, a rare breed that's going to establish a great nation. I wasn't born here, but I was baptized Catholic so I could have citizenship," I said. "But now I'm a Texican."

Many of the men nodded, as a murmur swept the room, Stetsons, sombreros, even a Scottish glengarry, all nodding.

"But when we're through, all of us—even you three—can bear the name Texican, because we earned it by fighting for that right," I continued. "Scot, Irish, Mexican, English, even Polacks and Jews. All of us."

Men continued to nod in agreement as hands moved back onto the bar or table to re-grasp beer mugs or shot glasses.

I felt Emily's eyes bore into me. I hadn't mentioned her kind, but I couldn't. Right now a debate raged in this country—hell, in Texas—over slavery. It would be another matter to be solve, hopefully without guns.

I nodded towards her. "Who knows, maybe even Emily's kind will one day know the glory of being Texican."

A negative rustle crossed the room as eyes turned her way. She offered a small smile and nod of the head.

I raised my hand. "Boys. Before you dismiss it, remember that Joe—Travis' slave—killed a couple of Santa Anna's men during the battle."

Still unhappy with the thought of a slave being their equal, a few of the men nodded. It was time to refocus the impromptu meeting.

"You came to me tonight spoiling for a fight, and almost took it out on each other instead of on Santa Anna's boys."

A bit guilty, they looked one to another. A Tennessee frontiersman in a coonskin hat and a Kentuckian in buckskins exchanged uneasy glances, then broad smiles.

"Damn straight," Mountain Man said. "But we're ready to put those Mexicans in their place. They got no right to our land. We paid for it with sweat and blood and their damn taxes."

Like Wellington taking on Napoleon, I had to retreat and then retreat some more until the time was right. Hell, I didn't know when it would be right. It was something better felt than told, but I'd know, and when I knew, we'd have our victory, even if we were outnumbered and out-supplied.

Instead, I told the men. "It may seem like a retreat to you, but I'm setting a trap for that pepperbelly poppycock who thinks he's the Napoleon of the West. When the time's right, we spring the trap."

I raised my glass. "Huzzah," I yelled.

A few answered.

"Huzzah," I yelled again.

This time the whole bar—including the terrible trio—chimed. All of us brothers, united against the Mexican menace, steadily slogging through the rain in pursuit of my brave Texicans.

Emily looked back, this time a full grin on her face, her hands on the bar, shaking her head at the scene.

CHAPTER THIRTY-ONE

A Call From The Secretary of State—March 28, 1836

As if combat wasn't hard enough, we had to contend with men who imagined themselves heads of state. And we had to pretend we were inviting them into quarters commensurate with their stations.

Truth was, it was still only a tent.

Reality is a hard Taskmaster sometimes. Emily had done her best to make it into a reception hall for dignitaries. Fresh bluebonnets and red Indian blankets floated in a bowl atop a trunk covered with my best quilt. Discretely-placed honeysuckle perfumed the air.

Straight back chairs faced each other for the big powwow. A small table, probably rescued from the refuse scattered along the Runaway Scrape trail, stood cleaned and polished. A bottle of wine stood alongside sliced apples and cheese and fried meat pies.

Thomas Jefferson Rusk, the infant republic's Secretary of War, was on his way, dispatched by that *watumka,* that old hog thief, David G. Burnet, who had wormed his way into the title of provisional president. I couldn't do both, so I'd selected the title of General, given the certainty that we'd be in worse shape than we were now if Burnet had this job.

A man of little personal merit, Burnet had been orphaned as a child and raised by his older half-brothers, and he was riding on his family's coattails. His father had served in America's Continental Congress, and another brother was a senator, and still another the mayor of Cincinnati. His failures in the North had driven him to Texas, where failure continued to be his companion. If that's not riding on coattails I didn't know what was.

He couldn't even succeed in challenging me to a duel. When his second arrived I sniffed, "I don't fight downhill" and sent him packing. That was the last I heard of that.

But my blood boiled when he spoke against independence last year. Eloquent. Sure, but with the forked tongue of a rattler. He wasn't even a delegate to the recent constitutional convention but through pure arrogance thrust himself into the thick of things, and that silver tongue won him the provisional presidency by seven votes.

Now he was going to try to tell me how to run this war. I'm in a retreat carrying half of Texas on my back, and he's out of harm's way moving the government from Washington-on-the-Brazos to Harrisburg to Galveston. I don't think he'll stop retreating till he hits the Gulf and can't go any farther.

Deef had brought me another jug of corn whiskey crafted by the rough hands of a farmer in Goliad. I took a swig, then grinned when I remembered Jim Bowie almost emptying one of these jugs when I convinced him to go to San Antonio to destroy the Alamo. Had he followed orders, destroyed it and left, he'd be alive today, along with Crockett and Travis. I could sure use these warriors. Instead, their ghosts will have to spur the living.

The raw whiskey went down so smoothly it took my breath away and I went into a coughing spasm.

"General, if you're going to drink with the big boys, you got to learn how to swallow." Deef laughed as he filled a glass with water and brought it to me. "This'll clear the cobwebs out of your throat. You gonna need those golden tones when Rusk gets here."

I pushed the water away and took another swig of the jug as the fiery liquid lit a golden glow in my gut.

Rusk had studied law in South Carolina. It was what had brought him to Texas. A group of men had cheated him out of a thousand dollars in the purchase of shares in a mineral and gold mine. He could have let the whole thing drop, chalked it up to experience. But not Rusk. He followed the men to Nacogdoches where he found out they had lost the money gambling. Only then did he give up the effort.

You could say it was love at first sight when Rusk crossed the Red River into Texas. The verdant grass and pine trees and azaleas won his heart, not to mention the rumblings of war and independence. He sent for his family. He organized a company of soldiers for the Texas Army. He and I signed the Declaration of Independence. Then I'd had to leave to get on to Gonzales to organize the army.

I took a swig, a little one this time, and it fueled the golden glow in me. This was powerful stuff. I had to be cautious or I might go too far, and this was not the time for that. My Cherokee brothers called me Big Drunk behind my back and I didn't want to prove them right at this critical time. I needed his good will. Besides, I had an ace in the hole.

"General." Emily's voice broke my reverie.

"The honorable Thomas Jefferson Rusk, secretary of war, is here to see you."

I rose as she escorted him in. Broad-faced, with a big nose and deep set eyes under bushy eyebrows, he brushed a dangling black cowlick off his forehead, grinned and extended his hand.

"General. It is a great honor. I have been looking forward to meeting the great Sam Houston. Your reputation precedes you."

He must have forgotten we met at Washington-on-the-Brazos or, as Burnet's emissary, he might be trying to warm me up for the bad news hovering on the horizon.

So, the greeting startled me. I cocked my head as I took his hand. Was he making a jest of me with this greeting or was it sincere?

The grip was firm, not strong. Was he testing me?

"Likewise," I said, deciding to test back. "How is that old *Watumka*, President Burnet?"

"*Watumka?* I don't believe I've ever heard that term, and he's doing quite well."

"It's just a form of endearment, an Indian expression I learned in my years with the Cherokee," I said, ready to switch the subject. "I believe you have something for me."

He reached into his breast pocket and pulled out an envelope. When he handed it to me without a word I noticed it bore the presidential seal in wax.

I motioned to the chairs at the table prepared with treats.

"You really don't take much time in preliminaries."

I broke the seal and opened the document. "You should try talking to the Cherokees. That's a combination of Sunday mass and a woman's sewing circle complete with gossip."

He laughed, a smile lighting up his round face.

I laid the letter down. "Before we go any further, Mr. Secretary." He threw up his hand, "Thanks for the courtesy, but it's just Tom, in here, between the two of us."

"Then I'd be happy to be Sam."

He nodded.

"There's someone I want you to meet."

On cue, Emily announced from the door "I'd like to introduce Charles Stanfield Taylor, a signer of the Texas Declaration of Independence."

We rose to greet the man I had met earlier that morning and learned of a delicate mission he'd undertaken. I'd missed him at Washington-on-the-Brazos by heading out for Gonzales immediately after signing the declaration earlier than he. He and Rusk knew Taylor from their years in Nacogdoches.

"Charlie. How are you? I was sorry to hear about your children."

"We were fortunate that only two of them died from exposure instead of all four," Taylor said. The family had fled East in the Runaway Scrape. He stood erect in our presences an able-bodied man with a high forehead, widespread eyes, a broad nose and friendly mouth. "Thank you. Their mother still grieves for them."

"Mr. Secretary, I'd like to make a presentation," he said without more preliminary conversation. He stepped forward and placed a heavy sack in Rusk's hands.

The secretary furrowed his brow.

In answer, Taylor added. "In the past I've been charged with collecting the taxes imposed by the Mexican government and forwarding it to them."

Rusk nodded as revelation brought a quick smile.

"These are the latest taxes, a sum that will not enrich Santa Anna's coffers, but will instead purchase bullets and cannon shot that will help enable our Texican boys to destroy him," he said, grinning back. Rusk hefted the bag. "A little over five thousand, mostly in silver coin and a few bills."

"That will supply a small army," Rusk said.

"Which we already have," I interjected.

"I need to get back to my wife. We have two other children to tend to," Taylor said.

Emily escorted Taylor out and I turned to Rusk.

"Well…?"

"I like you Sam, but you haven't read the letter yet."

I invited him to re-take a seat at the table and joined him to open the letter. An order to stop in my tracks and attack the Mexican forces.

"This is tomfoolery."

Rusk sat impassively, slowing chewing on a bite of apple. Outside I heard orders called out, a chorus of responses from troops—men going about the business of training for war. Inside, honeysuckle tickled my nose, along with the faint smell of an apple.

"Prove it." Rusk's tone changed from affable to argumentative.

Outside this tent marched the army of the Texas revolution. Mired in mud, challenged by unrelenting cold and skies that alternately dropped rain and a touch of snow. Only a few hundred men tramping around and snarling against their leader, many calling him—me—a coward, and, like Burnet, demanding that we strike now.

It seemed like half the people of Texas were fleeing east, seeking protection with us, Santa Anna on their heels, intermingling with my men and causing delays in training.

"Why can't you fight now?"

Maybe Rusk would understand what I was doing. Maybe he was a student of history and would understand Wellington and Napoleon. I assumed he knew of them, so I told him exactly what I was doing.

When I finished, most of the apple and cheese was gone, as was the wine. Rusk studied me, a long probing look, as if he wanted to enter my brain.

Finally, he spoke. "I also have a letter that gives me the power to replace you."

I felt the blood drain from my face as my pulse raced. I caught my breath, breathing slowly through my nose in an effort to control my raging body. He had seemed receptive to my plan, even asking intelligent questions. This last remark was an unexpected emotional blow to my solar plexus. I heard Emily's dress rustle in the background. It seemed she took a step then stopped.

So this was going to be the end.

He reached into his pocket and took the letter out, holding it up by one end.

"This authorizes me to replace you if I believe it should be done."

Rusk then tore it into two pieces. Placed them together and ripped again and again until there were only fragments, which he then tossed into the fire.

Rising he extended his hand, which I grabbed to make sure I didn't fall on buckling knees.

"Just call on me when you're ready to attack. I'll be there."

CHAPTER THIRTY-TWO

Torching San Felipe

Dear Mother,

You must be worried, not hearing from me for so long. In truth, I don't know that this will reach you, or if it does, how long it will take to find you.

Some time ago, I left Morgan's Point to transport some goods to a convention a few days distant. I met with a great many troubles on the way and am very fortunate that I lived to write this. I have great hopes of returning to you the free woman I was when I left, but I am now without papers in the land of slavers and I am terrified of falling into bondage. Only the patronage of General Houston protects me at the moment, and we are in great trouble and about to plunge into a fierce battle. . .

It had been three days since I'd started the letter, and still couldn't find the words to go on. I couldn't pass over everything that happened by talking of "many troubles." Yet, how could I describe what really happened without going into far more detail than she deserved to know? I tucked it in the pocket I'd sewed in my camisole, blew out the candle, and crawled under the covers beside the General.

He was quite a snorer, and I'd lost some sleep until I learned that a gentle push of a heel in the small of the back turned him over and quieted him. I snuggled up to his back and tucked my dress under my head for a pillow. This war trail didn't seem so bad at that moment.

I'd just drifted off, when he turned over. I did the same, and now he was at my back. He grunted and twisted some, and I knew I wouldn't be sleeping again for a while.

I had little basis for comparison of men in these situations. A servant boy, which hardly counted, since it was mostly a matter of curiosity and neither of us knew what went where and how and why, and it was over so quickly we both wondered what had happened. The village grocer's son seemed like love for a while, but that stream ran fast and not so deep. And now Houston.

Love is the first question in such situations, but I'd barely asked it when I realized it made no sense. You don't ask the sun or the moon or a hurricane about love. You don't question the right or wrong of them because they are Nature with ways beyond our ken, and so it was with Houston.

He could be gentle as a damselfly landing on a pond, kind of like the way he was nuzzling me right then, calling me "sweetness" as he'd been doing ever since that first night. Or he could charge like a bull moose, which might or might not happen later. Or he might choose something in between. It all depended on his mood, and—for the first time in my life I realized I had the power—on my mood as well. And it turned out my mood was more heated than I'd thought it would be, exhausted as I was. So we followed one another through the surges of our emotions and our bodies and before long I lay swaddled like a baby in one of his long-armed, long-legged, big-hearted embraces, making believe this would last forever.

***

I'd gotten used to the stink-eye from the other women as I went about my morning chores, and I paid them no mind. I'd trade that unpleasantness any day for my hours under Houston's blanket. And so would they. For once, it was not raining that morning. There was even some blue sky, and the sun shone down on San Felipe de Austin a mile so downstream from our camp on the east bank of the Brazos. We'd retreated from the Guadalupe, crossed the Colorado and now the Brazos. Three rivers behind us, and we still hadn't seen more than an occasional Mexican squadron. Much farther east, and we'd be in Louisiana. Even I was beginning to wonder when this runaway scrape of the General's would end.

Yesterday, as we finished crossing the Brazos, we all wondered at the stream of folks moving out of San Felipe. You could understand refugees from Apache attacks, but these families seem to be abandoning a perfectly good community. This morning, Houston had squeezed my shoulders, looked me in the eye and said, "It's going to be a sad day, Sweetness, and no help for it."

When I asked him what he meant, he told me to wait and see, and now I was beginning to understand. In the distance, I saw mounted Texicans with firebrands enter San Felipe. Then smoke began to rise out of the town into the morning sun. Soon you could see the flames that generated the smoke. Kitty Jo, Mary Rose, and I stood mute with our entire company, knowing that we were watching the first capital of Texas being put to the torch by her own people. Mary Rose started whimpering, turned her head away, and wrapped her arms around Kitty Jo. The next sentence in my letter to Mother came to me:

Is my General the creator or the destroyer of this new nation?

CHAPTER THIRTY-THREE

Freedom

I gave the order to burn San Felipe this morning. Had to, though it still hurts me to think of it. It was not a place to make our stand, and we couldn't afford to let Santa Anna have the spoils it offered. All in the cause of Texican Freedom. Freedom. Freedom. That multi-layered word.

To the Indians it is migrating across vast plains, in the temperate months following the path of buffalo and deer and water fowl. During the winter, taking advantage of the mild climates along the Arkansas River or the Rio Grande or an occasional canoe trip down the Mississippi River. No ploughed ground or fences to block the paths of the great humped beasts. To each Indian the land was his, as far as the eye could see.

Freedom to roam. And in just a few decades, the white man had trapped the beaver out of the mountains. Only a few buffalo herds remained, and the Indians had learned a new word—reservation.

Some of the best years of my life I spent in Indian camp running a general store with my now ex-wife, until Ol' Hickory called me to fetch Texas for him.

But it had turned into a difficult life for Chief Bowl and his people. I thought, as I often did, and as I'd reminded Chief Bowl, about the day I nearly beat a man to death for accusing me of bilking the Cherokees out of money. It turned into an assault charge, and I hired Francis Scott Key to defend me. But he was too drunk the day of the trial, so I did my own lawyering.

I learned a new meaning of freedom that day. If I hadn't won I would have gone to prison. So my personal freedom was in jeopardy, just as tyrant Santa Anna endangered the freedom of us Texicans.

If I lost this war, chances are I'd go to prison or be shot. Santa Anna gives no quarter. I couldn't wait to have him in my gunsights. Then he'd understand the full meaning of "no quarter."

"A penny for your thoughts."

Sweetness. There was no voice I'd rather have interrupt my brooding.

I had been staring into the campfire, huddled under a dirty quilt some woman had spent hours creating. The fat layer of cotton between the hand-pieced blocks did a decent job of warding off the cold, as long as it didn't get wet. Overhead, a tarpaulin rectangle stretched between mesquites, caught most of the chilling rain and channeled it down the sides. There weren't enough blankets to tie up for shelter. Every one was needed by the men.

It was about as dry and warm as this temperamental weather would give us. Mid-day had given us a break, coats were taken off to dry in the steamy sun until sunset and the return of rain.

"Not much."

"You were far away. Tell me where you were."

Sweetness had returned and sat next to me, our backs to a large wheel from a freight wagon. She shuddered. I opened my quilt and invited her in.

She hesitated.

"You mad at me again?"

"It's just it's out here in front of everyone. Shouldn't we go in the tent?"

"Get in here before I lose what little heat I have."

She slipped under the blanket and into my arms. I felt the essence of her body, warm and soft; and feminine, even in these godforsaken conditions. My manhood stirred. I chuckled.

"What's so funny?" she said.

"Me…you… us."

She cocked her head, and a cold nose brushed my cheek. I pulled the bandana off my neck, folded it into a robber's mask and tied it around her head like a drover fighting dust on a cattle drive.

"The warmth of your breath will heat your face."

"Thank you." A muffled sound as her hand sought mine under the covers. It was cold. Her fingers turned warm under my massage.

"You never answered my question."

She could be frustrating, unwilling to let go, like a blue-tick hound worrying a bone.

"I was thinking about freedom."

"Freedom?" she said.

"It's why we're here, after all, isn't it? In this war?"

"Is it?"

"Why else, Emily?" She looked at me sort of sideways and pulled away. I was puzzled for a moment, then something about her look brought me up short. I was holding a woman I called "Sweetness," but who much of the rest of the world called merely "slave" or worse. My next thought frightened me. Had all those fervent kisses and sweet caresses been pleasures of passion or simply the blind duty of a slave girl? I mentally slapped my own hand for doubting her.

"I'm fine right here, Sam. But you're all that stands between me and those bounty hunters and their kind. My freedom seems anything but secure."

"I think freedom is where you find it, Sweetness, and we've found it here and now under this quilt."

The here and now is not forever," she said.

"But it's all we have, isn't it?" I whispered.

I pulled her to me, planted a soft kiss on her lips. "And you're all I need." It felt almost true.

CHAPTER THIRTY-FOUR

Whichaway Tree

Sometimes there are small moments in life. The smell and soft pop of bubbling stew rekindling the sometimes-forgotten wonder of mother's love. Soft candle light playing games with shadows. Chinked logs holding the bitter spring rains at bay. The comfort of an overstuffed chair that chases away the pain of an old war wound in your shoulder. The peace of solitude as the world roars around you.

"General."

And then there's Emily. Not Emmy or any other nickname, although I find the working girls' tag of Dragon Lady to be accurate with her stern rules to protect them. Or Shylock, her name when working with Dr. Morgan's debtors.

However, to me, she was my Sweetness.

"General, you asleep?"

I kept my eyes closed listening to the rustle of her dress as she crossed the room. Her hand touched my forehead, warm, no doubt, from washing dishes at the bar.

"No." I kept my eyes closed, summoning a picture of her in my mind. She stood tall, dressed in a shimmering golden ball gown highlighted with threads of purest silver from Bowie's lost mine. Tiny feet were covered with shoes the color of fading prairie grass in the fall. A tiara, aflame with diamonds, sparkled on her curly black hair. Her brown skin glowed in the flickering yellow light. She was my very own Sleeping Beauty, who had already awakened me to a new world of possibilities, and was ready to go to the ball.

She shook my shoulder and I grabbed her arm to whip her into my lap as the old chair groaned from the additional weight.

"General!"

We kissed. Soft, long and when we pulled apart I could feel her breath rush into me, a living legacy of love.

"I told you not to call me that in private. You can call me Samuel or Sam or even Sammy, but not general, not in private," I said, putting my finger over her lips to block a protest.

My lap held a different version of Emily. A tattered dish towel swept her hair back, although it was still ringlets. A simple peasant dress in dark brown—the better to hide stains with she told me—was covered with a tattered and stained white cloth serving as an apron. Work boots stuck out from under the dress.

I laughed. "What's so funny?"

"The difference between fantasy and reality."

"Well, then, my mythical Raven, you'd better get it straight, and get it fast. I thought we were about to go to war amongst ourselves a while ago," she said. "Those men are spoiling for a fight, not a Runaway Scrape."

"I told you—and them—we're not running away. We're retreating. And when the time and the place is right, then we'll engage in battle," I said.

She studied me, tracing a tiny scar on my face, just one of the souvenirs of the Battle of New Orleans. President Jackson—then a General—led a rag-tag group to victory; me and my small group, privateer Jean Lafitte and his band of sea-going marauders, and the general with his regular army. It had been a glorious day, the day we pushed the British out of the Crescent City and secured the future of the United States.

I could sure use Lafitte now, but his Galveston paradise had been shut down and he was at sea running for his life from the very nation he helped save.

"You've saved one nation, now you're trying to found another," she said.

"I feel like the general must have with his motley crew. I've read his account of the battle. He said that he led 'an infamous army, very weak and ill-equipped.' I know how he felt. All I have are kids wet behind the ears, farmers, ranchers, butchers, cowhands, vaqueros, hell, I've even heard a woman was found dressed like a man. They should have left her be. I can use all the help I can get."

"Including the three slave-trading trouble makers?"

"I know it bothers you, but they can shoot and bleed and die for a good cause, just like the others."

"And if they ever find out where Joe went, they'll light out looking for him."

I nodded.

"When will you take a stand?"

"I don't know Sweetness."

"The talk among the men is that you're heading toward the American border at Louisiana. They believe you plan to take refuge there, not fight." She paused. "Now don't go getting red-faced on me." Taking my face in both hands, she brought her face scant inches from my own. "Some even say you're a coward."

Blood pounded in my ears. I thought my head was going to explode. I took a deep breath. She wouldn't let go of my face. For an instant I felt a flash of hate that anyone—especially her—would challenge my manhood.

"I know you're not. But you need to know this. You need to do something."

"I am. We're in a strategic retreat. Just like the Duke of Wellington, when he defeated Napoleon at the Battle of Waterloo. Many of his men thought he was a coward, too, but the Duke was smarter than Napoleon."

I stopped when Sweetness knitted her eyebrows, fear pulling the corner of her lips down. My blood was pounding in my ears.

"There's no reason to shout," she said quietly.

I put my hands over hers. They were warm and soft from just washing the bar dishes.

"Shhhh, Sam. Take another deep breath."

I did. My heart eased its pounding, the desire to leap up and fight, to throw the furniture, anything to ease my temper.

"And another."

Soon I was breathing slowly, my body relaxing.

"You've got to promise me when you go into battle you won't lose it like this. Don't let your temper defeat you."

I took her hands off my cheeks and cradled them.

"Santa Anna thinks of himself as the Napoleon of the West, a title some newspaper editor hung on him and this two-bit tyrant's ego exploded. I'll admit it didn't take much, but this Napoleon is only a few days from meeting his Waterloo.

"A year before the battle Wellington had scouted a spot in case he needed it to prepare an attack," I said. "Don't forget I've spent many years here. I know the land well."

"You know where to attack?"

"I have an idea. If Santa Anna will cooperate."

***

Getting Santa Anna to cooperate was one thing. Getting my Texicans to cooperate was quite another. On they slogged, discontent growing by the moment. I kept promising hope by the minute, but delivering little to base it on. The legendary Whichaway Tree, which was to be our guide to victory. Did it even exist? Many had ceased to believe in it any more than they believed in elves and fairies. I was beginning to wonder myself. Then, finally, we reached a bend in the trail, and suddenly there it was. One limb pointed north toward the

Louisiana border. Home and safety. The other south, toward battle and bloodshed and victory.

A two-wheel wagon seemed to float atop the muddy terrain as the driver turned north. A deep voice floated on the air. "Maybe that Sam Houston ain't ready to fight Santa Anna, but I damn sure am."

"Me, too."

"Me, too."

A chorus arose. "Well let's take the decision away from him." Then another voice sang out. I recognized him as a veteran soldier called One-eyed Jack.

"To the right, boys." He was standing at the base of the tree. "To the right, boys and Ol' Sam'll lead you to some big fight."

He began a singsong not unlike an auctioneer. Other voices joined in. "To the right, boys." Before I realized it he added his own voice, now shouting with a full-throated chorus that'd make the Galveston opera house proud. We were headed where I wanted, without exhortation from me.

"To the right, boys. . ." Righteousness shot through my body as my heart filled to bursting. The moment would be more complete only if Sweetness were there to share it with me. Then I heard her clear sweet soprano winging atop the manly chorus.

CHAPTER THIRTY-FIVE

The General In His Cups

Sweetness had more unadulterated gall than any man in either army, even Erastus. She stood on her toes, ready to flee if necessary, but still holding her ground. She held the last jug of moonshine Deef had brought me from Goliad on one of his scouting trips.

I felt the boiling blood of rage rush to my head. Swallowing hard, I said. "What are you doing, girl?" And the "girl" was the same word she heard in the taverns. I might as well have hit her as hurl that word at her with a drunken voice sharp as a tavern dart.

"I'm saving you." Tears drained down her cheeks as she swallowed hard, shoving the words through tightly clamped lips. I could see her teeth pushing down on the top lip.

She paused. "And I'm saving Texas."

"That's pretty arrogant. I don't need saving. How would you save Texas? Hell, you didn't even know how to shoot."

"I'm going to save the future of you both. Tonight."

She threw the jug to the floor, shattering the crockery jug. Long arms of liquid lashed out across the floor onto my moccasins and the edge of Emily's dress.

"Damn, girl. These moccasins were made for me . . ."

"I know. …By Chief Bowl's granddaughter. You've told me often enough."

That stunned me. Always, she had earned her nickname. Now Sweetness didn't seem the right one now. Shrew might fit her better tonight. That was the last of the crock jugs Erastus brought back from scouting trips. I'm not a superstitious man, but shattering a jug on the eve of battle against the men who murdered those gallant warriors at Goliad was a terrible omen.

Emily stood her ground, the shards of crockery sprayed across the earthen floor like so many soldiers fallen in battle.

"General. You are drunk."

I leapt to my feet to stagger the few feet toward her before she caught me. She nodded toward the bed. We stumbled to it. With a shove she threw me onto the bed. I landed on my front, and bounced to my back, heaving for breath, then heaving the barbecued pork she had prepared for me.

"You still think you're not drunk?"

"What makes you an expert? There must of been something in that meal you made me."

"First off, I ate the same meal. I'm fine. Second, I've handled so many men in their cups that you are child's play, Although it was a big disappointment to find out they were right when they called you 'big drunk.'"

My head shot up. How did she know that? I thought I left that name behind with the Indians.

"I know a lot more about you than you think, Mister Big Drunk Big Shot. Right now you need to get some coffee down you, control your horrible temper and leave the liquor alone till you've won the victory."

I rose to my knees, thought of jumping to my feet, but didn't think I'd make it. I pointed a finger at her, a speech prepared, but somehow it swam away, and all I managed was, "You. . . You. . . You. . ."

Then she took the sting out a bit by getting down on her knees and looking me in the eye.

"After that," she said. "Then I'll have one with you."

Another wave bolted out of my boiling stomach and undigested rotgut shot across the room leaving my digestive track scalded and my sinuses burning like hellfire.

Emily ran to me with a wet wash cloth. She put it on my head.

"Be careful you don't get any of that in your shoulder wound. No telling what it'd do to it, although as rancid as that stuff is, it might heal it."

She washed my face as I heaved without producing a thing. I lay there, limp as the wash rag she was using. Maybe it was all gone. No it wasn't, and I heaved again.

"Now, now, General. It's going to be okay. In a few minutes I'll get us some coffee. We'll drink it together and remember the good times and talk of future plans and good times."

How do you answer such cheerfulness when your whole world is collapsing?

She stared at me, then said the oddest thing. "When you remember Emily West, Sam Houston, remember that whatever else happens, Emily West loves you. I love you."

I passed out only to awaken a few hours later, my head a bit clearer, including my wits. Emily sat across the way holding a cup of coffee. From the steam curling up I suspect she had just set it down.

"Are you feeling better my General?"

"Sam," I growled. "Call me Sam."

"Okay then…Sam. Are you feeling any better?"

"I feel like I've taken a beating and like someone stuffed my mouth full of cotton," I said. For some reason I didn't want to say "shit." It didn't seem appropriate in her company, although I knew she'd heard much worse.

She sat her cup down, rose and went to the indoor campfire at the edge of the tent and poured me a cup, then she slipped a flask out of her blouse and poured some of it into my coffee.

Emily smiled her Sweetness smile. "A little bit of the hair of the dog that bit you. Although this dog is a bit smoother."

I never knew she carried a flask. I wondered what else I didn't know about this unique woman.

"It's about four o'clock in the morning. We have plenty of time to clear your head."

I started to shake it, but a wave of nausea swept over me and a thunderbolt struck my head.

"Take it easy, Sam. You were on the way to a drunk to end all drunks."

"How'd you know I was called Big Drunk when I lived with the Cherokee?"

"You forgot that it was Chief Bowl who rescued me and handed me over to you. Those Cherokees have really loose tongues when they drink like they did during the celebration at Gonzales." Her tone was light, but her eyes heavy, carrying a burden that I should be sharing.

"I'm…" How the hell do you apologize? Many men have apologized to me, even when I was in the wrong. It's the Houston way. You plow straight through, don't look right or left, and always maintain control; in my case, even when I was drunk, perhaps, especially when I was drunk.

I patted the bed. She just rocked, studying me, deep in thought, she tried to hide the pain in her eyes.

"So, you think I should show you mercy, do you, Sam? You treated me like the lowest form of scullery maid while you were drunk, then expect me to clear your conscience with a simple 'That's all right.' Well, Samuel Houston, lord of the domain, it's not all right," she said, tears coming down her cheeks.

I patted the sheets again. "I'm still too wobbly to come to you."

She wiped the tears, went to get her another coffee. "You want more?" I heard the tears and hurt that she had borne all night.

"Yes, please."

She returned with another cup for me, the aroma even more appearing than before. When she handed it to me, I patted the sheets again, and she daintily sat down, as far from me as possible.

"Sweetness, I'm sorry…I didn't mean to hurt you."

"Did you hear that?" She turned her head around the room as if there was an audience.

"I…love you." The words rushed out in a tangled web.

"What did you say Samuel?"

I resented her school marm sound.

"I didn't quite get it. And, are you sober enough to say those words. You've never said them before."

"Okay. Okay. Okay. We're headed for the biggest battle of my life, so I figured it was time to . . .time to. . .let you know. . .Oh, hell." I threw my arms in the air.

"How about a toast?" she said softly.

"To what?" I said

"To a new nation." She lifted her coffee cup. "And a new us." Then she shoved herself full length into my arms, the hot coffee spilling onto the bed. I let out a yelp and she covered my mouth with a kiss.

"Don't be such a wimp," she whispered as she melted into my arms.

CHAPTER THIRTY-SIX

Intrigue at San Jacinto

Sunrise. And even after perhaps our most glorious night together, the general had left the tent already before I could talk to him, but I knew it was no use asking him anyway. After all the retreating and burning, we were finally on the verge of the battle that would decide the whole thing once and for all. The General had been very close-mouthed about his battle plans, but whatever they were, he would never allow me to try what I had in mind. I'd run over the conversation in my mind dozens of times.

"You need information, General. You say it yourself all the time. You can't attack without it." I'd say.

"Not that way, Sweetness," he'd reply.

"Then how?"

"We have scouts."

"About as quiet as cows in a thicket. You say it yourself all the time."

"Not now, Emily. We've got him where we want him."

"Then why haven't you attacked? You've been drilling and drilling all the way from that plantation and Harrisburg. And here Toño's right in front of you and still you wait. No wonder the men are so angry at you."

"Are you on their side now?"

And I'd never been able to imagine a better outcome to that talk, so it was up to me. Houston's victory was up to me. The future of Texas was up to me. I wrapped myself in all those high-sounding words, but underneath it all was this: If I was ever going to see my money or my mother again, If I was to avoid being bought and sold like a dog, Houston had to win, and I had to do whatever I could to make sure he did. First, however, I had to add what I hoped would not be the last paragraph to the long letter I'd been composing to my mother. It had grown to a veritable sheaf of papers by this time. Whether it would be delivered was questionable, but nature demanded that I write it nevertheless.

Dear Mother,

We are on the eve of a battle that will probably decide whether you and I ever see one another again. Know that I am full of love and gratitude for you every moment of every day and that I am doing my best to live up to everything you taught me. Let us both pray that we embrace once again on this earth and can tell one another all that has transpired since we parted so long ago.

And then I wrote my note to Sam Houston:

General

You've got over three hundred yards of open bayou to parade your men across before they fight. You need every edge you can get, so I'm going back into the camp to entice Toño into his tent for an afternoon of pleasure. Maybe his sentries will decide to take a siesta. It's a small price to pay for victory and freedom.
Attack when you see my pantaloons hanging outside his tent.
Whatever happens, remember that you, Sam, are the love of my life.
Sweetness

I had to get it to Sam, but not soon enough to give him a chance to stop me. But not too late, either, so he wouldn't miss my signal. I looked all over for Joe, but couldn't find him, figured he must be out drilling with the soldiers. That left only one person I could trust, and leaving it with him was almost as bad as approaching the general himself.

Deef Smith stood on a rise of ground, pacing, raising his glass from time to time like a lookout on deck of a ship. I took a deep breath and approached him.

"Mr. Smith." I had to say it twice, of course. He turned to me, giving me that serpent's look he reserved especially for me.

"I'm busy, missy."

"And am I. So let's not waste time bantering. I need you to get this confidential message to the general within the hour."

He looked at the envelope, but made no move to accept it. "I'm your errand boy now?" he said.

I took another deep breath. Flattery was a sure tactic with almost any man, but how I hated to resort to it with one I so despised. Yet, circumstances demanded it.

"No," I said. "But you are General Houston's right hand man and the only one to be trusted with such a dispatch in this crucial hour."

He took the envelope. Nodded, but said nothing. I don't know quite what possessed me to humble myself so, but I actually curtsied as I thanked him. Then I turned and fairly ran back down the hill. My heart jumped when I heard his voice call out behind me.

"Stop her." Two sentries responded instantly, one on each arm. I twisted and objected, but they held firm. Smith approached shortly, waving the unsealed note as he came.

"I said that note was confidential." I fairly spat the words at him.

"Ah, but I am the General's right hand man, ain't I? So a message to him is same as a message to me, ain't it?"

"You know very well—"

"Shut yer pie hole, hussy." His face was close enough that I could have counted his whiskers, and his hand was raised. But he didn't dare use it and let it drop directly. "Tie her up good," he said. "The wheel of that wagon she's so proud of should work like a charm. And don't worry, Miss Emily, your ladyship … " he executed a mock imitation of my curtsy. "I'll make sure this gets to the General's own hand directly."

***

It wasn't long before I was snugged up against the spokes of the wagon wheel just as Smith had ordered. The sentries returned to their posts, sure they'd done their job well enough to give me no chance of escape. I twisted till my wrists were raw, desperate and angry. Passersby either dared not help me or were glad for my fix. A few even spat at me. For a time, a small crowd gathered, but with the battle seemingly imminent, there were too many urgent tasks at hand to spend much time on me.

I knew Houston would be furious at what Smith had done, but trussed and gagged like this, there seemed nothing to do but wait till he discovered me himself, something that could take hours. I longed see his eyes, hear his voice. Then came a voice that was nearly as welcome.

"Emily, for god's sake, what's going on?"

He removed the gag as he spoke, and the second I could speak, I said, "Joe Travis, you are my savior."

CHAPTER THIRTY-SEVEN

Eve of the Battle— April 20, 1836

It had been a hard slog south from San Felipe, with a brief respite at the Groce plantation. Deef Smith came galloping up, holding the reins to horses carrying two Mexican pepperbellies resplendent in their new royal blue uniforms, hands tied, eyes bulging.

I knew the Napoleon of the West was right behind us. I just didn't know how far. Santa Anna himself was in command of this column. He had burned Harrisburg. We saw the smoke. He then ordered his troops down the west side of the bayou which kept them on the west bank of the San Jacinto River where they crossed over the bridge at Vince's Bayou. He was so close it was a wonder I hadn't been smelling garlic in the air.

He had marched into a virtual trap surrounded on three sides by the San Jacinto River and watery bayous. The only way out of this predicament for the Mexicans was for them to re-cross the bridge. But weeks of rain had swollen the small creek into a roiling torrent. Why he would put himself into such a position was hard to figure. Was he setting a trap, or had someone just given him bad information?

"Burn Vince's Bridge," I ordered.

"Yes, sir," Deef said, wheeling his horse, as he called out to fellow calvarymen. "Alsbury, Coker, Garner, Lapham, Rainwater. Reaves. Come on boys." The men spurred their horses after their leader.

"Well, boys," I said to the few dozen surrounding me. "It looks like we're about to fulfill your wishes. In a matter of hours it will be victory for us and we'll drive these devils out of our beloved Texas." They cheered. My stomach churned, the old wound I got fighting for Old Hickory started to ache. I wish I had as much faith in my words as these men did.

A clatter of hooves, and in rode Big Foot Wallace herding a pair of trussed up Mexican soldiers.

"Got a couple of beaners here for you, general." There was a big smile on his face.

"*El Jefe,*" one whispered, rolling his eyes to the heavens. "*Madre de dios*, we are dead."

I pulled my pistol, eased my horse next to him and planted the barrel in his ear. Grease from the slicked down hair mingled with sweat running in small rivulets down the side of his face. He said something I didn't understand, so I looked at Bigfoot, a goofy grin creasing his beard.

"Before you kill 'em, he wants to see a priest."

I shook my head. Let him go straight to hell and skip Purgatory, a place I didn't much believe in anyway.

"*Por favor, Jefe.*" His mouth was so dry he barely got the words out.

"Wallace, you tell him to tell us where his heathen boss is." I paused. "And I want to know if he was at the Alamo or Goliad."

Both recognized Alamo and Goliad and the voice of the one with the pistol in his ear began to shriek. "No Alamo. No Goliad. No Alamo. No Goliad." Soon the other joined him. By now I had a small group surrounding me.

"You damn liars," I said, barely able to keep from killing them on the spot.

Wallace shifted in his saddle, a knife suddenly in his hand. He put it to the throat of the other captive, who began to bawl like a baby.

Reports were that Santa Anna showed no quarter, so he expected none, and suddenly the dam opened, each trying to out-talk the other to save his own life.

I was in no mood to listen. Take 'em into the woods where their worthless corpses won't be in the way," I ordered.

"Gladly, General, gladly," Bigfoot said.

In short order we silently advanced until we could see the Mexican camp across Buffalo Bayou, high and dry and well-fortified. We faded into the woods, setting up camp about three-quarters of a mile from their camp where breastworks of trucks, baggage, pack-saddles and other equipment faced the bayou. To get to them we had to cross more than three hundred yards of open bayou filled with deadly critters and dangerous sink holes.

***

We spent a restless night and I wrote a couple of dispatches. One to my good friend Henry Raguet. I wanted it on the record, so I told Henry that we were preparing to attack. "It is the only chance for saving Texas."

The other I addressed to the People of Texas.

"We view ourselves on the eve of battle. We are nerved for the contest, and must conquer or perish… We must act now or abandon all hope."

It was our moment in history. It would be remembered with glory and the establishment of a great nation, or one of the worst defeats in the history of mankind.

I called Bigfoot to me. The day before, a boat of contraband, including supplies and meat, had been captured; probably plunder from Harrisburg or New Washington.

"Break out the supplies. Fill the men with a good breakfast. Make it a feast." He nodded. For some of these Texicans it would be a last supper.

I could see Santa Anna's flags mocking us over the enemy camp on Texican land. Bugle calls echoed over the bayou, strident, braying a challenge; perhaps the famous "No quarter" that bounced off the walls of the Alamo. With the exception of the roar of battle, the last sound on the ears of so many brave men. My subordinates have been agitating for a fight. By damn they'd get it now.

I called for a council of war with my lieutenants. Present was Thomas J. Rusk, secretary of war, who had just arrived that day. Interim President Burnet had sent him to urge me to attack. Now he could turn in his own report. Also attending were Colonels Edward Burleson and Sidney Sherman, Lieutenant Colonels Henry Millard, Alexander Somervell and Joseph L. Bennett, and Major Lysander Wells.

Ignoring the rain, the men gathered outside the command tent. Colonel Sherman sat astride his battle mount, idly stroking the animal's neck. Major Wells sat whittling against the oak that give us some protection from the downpour. Colonel Millard stood clenching and unclenching his hands into balled fists, a prize fighter ready to leap into battle. I asked each to give an assessment. All but two wanted to wait for Santa Anna to attack us. That was a far cry from what the men in the ranks wanted.

I kept my own counsel. There was plenty of opinion out there and had I listened to them all, I'd become the ass standing between mouth-watering stacks of hay, not knowing which to eat first and starving to death. So, I consulted no one—with the the exception of Emily. This was my first council of war. If I erred, the blame would be all mine. I pretty much had the plan worked out, until Emily pulled her stunt.

Deef rode up and reined in his snorting horse. He was breathless.

"Vince's Bridge has been burned. The Mexicans have no way to retreat," he said.

"Neither do we," Sherman said, before hastily adding. "But the victors have no need for retreat."

Deef rolled his eyes to one side, calling me for a private conference, since his scouting rank didn't allow him access to the full conference. A second head roll told me it was important enough to stall the conference further.

"Give me a minute," I told the men, then walked to Deef's snorting stallion. He eased the animal further from the conference, before bending over, his face only inches from my ear.

"I think that gal of yours is about to walk into a Mexican hell." He handed me a folded note in Emily's flowery hand, mute testimony to the care she had in early childhood. "I think she's going into that devil's camp to try and distract him so you can attack." He was a bit embarrassed. "Actually, I know she is. She told me and told me to give you this note. Nothing I said would change her mind. She was hellbent on doing it, so I tied her up so you could talk to her. She gave me that note when she thought I was going to let her walk off. You better talk to her."

Tarnation. All I needed was a stubborn woman just a few hours before battle. Without a word to my lieutenants I jumped on my horse and followed Deef. When we got there, she was gone. Just some lengths of rope hanging on the wagon wheel where Deef said he'd left her. I told Deef to find her. Then I read her note.

I leaned against the wagon wheel where she'd been recently tied and tried to think. Trembling hands folded and refolded the notes, flashes of anger raged across my chest so that one moment I could breathe, the other choked for breath.

The raw images of what Santa Anna would soon be doing to the sweetest rose of Texas brought the taste of egg and bacon to my throat and I choked on the breakfast she'd cooked me that morning. Then fury shook me like a willow in a windstorm, my body trembled with rage, my hands shook, heat radiated off my face. I knew I would explode. But I had to control my emotions. Her decision would affect my battle plans if she made it into the Mexican camp. Just as my head was clearing, Deef came back to the tent.

"I couldn't find her, General. I guess she made it across."

"Find a tall oak, one where you can see Santa Anna's tent." Waving the note at him, I added, "Watch for a pair of pantaloons on the tent pole. That means she made it into his tent and they're ripe for our attack. I've got to get back to the council."

"General? You want me to go shinny up a tree?"

"You know what's in the note. We don't want to miss the signal."

"Aye, aye, sir." He always acknowledged a command he didn't like with a nautical term.

I locked his eyes with a steely stare. "I don't like it either." I mounted my horse and turned to leave.

"General." I twisted in my saddle to face him. "She's a good soldier."

I nodded. It was about noon. We probably had about three hours to prepare the attack. I put aside my fear and fury about Sweetness and headed back to the council.

CHAPTER THIRTY-EIGHT

Return to Toño

It was partly an act of gratitude, partly one of strategy when I passed my savings on to Joe.

"Why were you tied up, Emily?" he asked me. I explained. "You're planning to go over there?" He pointed the Mexican camp.

"I have to, Joe. What about you?"

"Guess I'm about to help finish what we started at the Alamo," he said.

"Let me give you another choice," I said. "Come on."

The General's tent was guarded, but the sentries knew me and knew nothing of what Smith had done, so getting inside, even with Joe beside me presented no difficulty. Lined up in the back of the tent, Houston kept three identical brass and leather chests, each substantially padlocked. One of them held his cash, the other two nothing but rocks. He switched the contents regularly like a sidewalk shell game. Then he buried the keys next to a different tent peg every night, keeping the earth dug to appear the same in each location. It wouldn't stop a determined burglar, but unless someone was as knowledgeable as I was, even if they disabled the sentry, it would cost some time to get to what they wanted, and that time was liable to be enough to get them caught. It was the best security he could manage in the field, he said.

I, of course, went directly to the keys and to the right trunk. The leather bag with my savings lay undisturbed. I handed it to Joe.

"What's this?" he asked.

"I was putting this away for my trip home. You rescued me. It's yours."

"But you're in as much trouble as I am."

"I have Houston, Joe. He can protect me. You have no one. You can buy your freedom with this. Take it with my thanks."

He didn't want to. Started several times to give it back, but I think the very thought of escape made it impossible for him to let go of that handful of liberation. His eyes grew wet.

"You know who you are? You ain't Emily, you're a yellow rose is what you are. A sweet flower in full bloom."

He took my hand, squeezed it hard, and fled from the tent.

I felt some regret at letting go of all that I'd worked so hard for, but I had no time to brood over it.

***

It wasn't hard to get past the sentries. Once beyond them, though, my way was uncertain. The Mexican army camp lay no more than a mile or so away and in plain sight, but this was bayou country, swampy and treacherous. If you strayed from the beaten path, you ran a good chance of falling into a muddy, bottomless hole or meeting up with a bad-tempered cottonmouth.

I was able to follow a trail for a couple of hundred yards, but I ran out of landmarks after that, and all I could to was test each step before I put my weight down. At one point, though, thinking about what I'd do when I encountered Toño, I stepped forward without testing properly, and found myself with one leg knee deep in quicksand. Off-balance, I tipped sideways off the narrow trail into a palo verde, which saved me. I hauled myself out of trouble. *Keep your mind on the job, child,* chided my mother's voice. How many times she had reminded me, and still I needed her correction. Just when I thought I was all grown up.

Finally, I approached my goal, and was surprised to see the laxness of Santa Anna's security. Sentries were spaced far apart, and several of them seemed to be leaning up against trees and dozing. I noticed liquor jugs on the ground. Although my knowledge of military matters was admittedly limited, such carelessness seemed to violate common sense, let alone Santa Anna's sense of discipline. Perhaps his long march had taken its toll on his alertness. I wondered what had happened to Sergeant Sanchez after Colleen and I had escaped. But no dwelling on that. The time had come to step back into the tiger's mouth.

"*Hola, señores,* I called as I raised my hands in the air.

"*Alto!*" came the expected answer. I did halt for a moment, but only long enough for them to get a look at me. A wet and bedraggled woman they might or might not recognize from days past.

"*Soy amiga,*" I said. Whether they recognized me or not, they probably wouldn't believe I was a friend, but I knew my next words would get me what I wanted. "*Traigame a* Toño, *por favor.*" The muskets lowered, and there followed a conversation I couldn't quite follow, but I could tell it was full of questions. A soaked and dirty wretch rising from the swamps and speaking of their commander in such intimate terms was bound to confuse them. In the end, though, they did what I knew they must and escorted me to Santa Anna's tent.

I stood outside and listened to muffled voices from within. It began to rain suddenly and in bucketfuls. The sergeant beside me remained at attention, water pouring off the bill of his hat. I notice his rifle was a cap and percussion model, probably one of the ones stolen from our wagons, so he made no move to keep his powder dry or water out of his barrel.

I began shivering, and my legs ached. My muscles were firm and well-conditioned from the hard work of the expedition, but something about my hike through the marshlands had weakened me. I resisted the impulse to hug myself for warmth and remained straight and tall as my guard while we waited and waited.

Finally, a private pulled the flap aside, and Santa Anna stood before me, his uniform coat unbuttoned, looking stern and angry. I threw myself at his feet, hugging his knees, weeping real tears, for I was truly miserable by that time.

"Toño, *mio. Lo siento mucho. Perdoneme. Perdoneme, por favor.*" He was struggling some to free his legs. Perhaps he wanted to kick me. He was certainly capable of that, and I had angered him greatly. I hugged him the tighter, and lifted my eyes to his, putting on as pleading look as I could muster. "I made such a mistake, Toño. I know I don't deserve it, but if you allow me back, you'll never regret it."

He quit struggling, then. "I have regretted I ever met you, Emily, ever since a certain night on the Colorado River. Why would I change my feelings now?"

I stood then, knowing I had accomplished the first part of my plan. I slid my hand inside his tunic and whispered. "Because I have just come from Sam Houston's camp, and I can tell you much."

The downpour stopped, and a benevolent sun shone down on the moment.

***

Santa Anna's attentions that afternoon were rougher than any I remembered, his intimacies accompanied by slaps and punches and curses. I didn't beg for mercy, though. I told him I understood his anger, that I deserved it all and more besides. By the time he finished, we were both exhausted and fell asleep at one another's side as if we were truly lovers.

Before we began, though, I'd begged relief from the sorry condition of my attire. With the encampment in such disarray, if Houston was ever going to prove his word to his army after all the running away, now was the time.

Santa Anna provided me with a wrap, and because I said I preferred to do the task myself, I hung my garments on poles outside his tent.

Most prominent—the pantaloons. If Deef had given him my note, the General would know what to do.

CHAPTER THIRTY-NINE

The Battle of San Jacinto

Emily pretty much changed my plan of action. After the debate at my war council, I thought it might be best to wait and attack first thing in the morning, while the Mexicans were having *frijoles* and tortillas. I'd have my men stock up on *fajitas* made of beef and tortillas and eat them cold before dawn. To any pepperbelly watching us with a spyglass we would still be asleep.

Now, if Emily's plan worked, she'd have Santa Anna in his tent doing who knows what to her, and perhaps his sentries—seeing their *Jefe* enjoying the pleasures of the flesh—might decide to take a nap. Knowing her, I'd bet she would encourage him to do just that.

Raw bumps washed over my body when a picture flushed through my mind, a vivid painting of what was going on inside that tent, only it was in living color, not black and white. An icy sliver shimmied across those bumps and my body felt hot and cold at the same time. My face flushed hot. I don't know if from anger or shame at what I conjectured.

I shook my head, like a dog shaking water after a swim, to clear it of those images and concentrate on the moment. Truth be told. Thousands of Texicans—women and children home working the farm with the elderly, deprived of the work usually provided by my men—were depending on me keeping a clear head. As I neared my tent, I was almost ready to curse the day we met.

I rode into a mess.

"Then what the hell are we doing traipsing around all over Texas in rain and mud if it's not to win independence from Mexico?" Sherman was saying.

"I agree." Mirabeau B. Lamar had joined the group. He was a new to this select group. I wasn't happy to see the two in cahoots. I had heard rumors that Sherman had suggested replacing me in a bloodless coup. I needed to put a stop to that talk. I needed every fighting man I could keep, so I challenged them: "Anybody tries to remove me from this command, I'll execute 'em on the spot." That seemed to control Sherman, but if he could enlist a man like Lamar into his camp, the tide could change.

Just the night before, Lamar had rescued two men from the Mexicans, and I'd promoted him from private to colonel on the spot. They had been caught in a skirmish launched by Sherman on a fool's errand that had almost brought on a full clash with Santa Anna prematurely.

The men fell silent as I rode into camp. "So you want to attack now?"

"Yes, sir," Lamar snapped. "Right now, as soon as possible."

"Then you're going to get your wish, Lamar, and you're going to be in charge of the cavalry." I saw him flinch. He'd expected to be given command of a full regiment. But he said nothing.

I had spent hours considering the battle plan. We crowded into the command tent, and I laid out the map. The men gathered round the small table as I unfurled a map.

"Lamar, you will bring the cavalry out on our right flank," I said, pointing to the road that led to now-smoldering Vince's bridge. "You will charge into their left flank, sort-of making a loop around into their camp.."

He grinned, relishing the challenge. I thought I'd taken some of the sting out of my previous rebuke. "All sixty-one of us, sir."

"Millar's Texas Regulars will fight next to you."

I marked two Xs in the middle of the battlefield, dividing the battlefield in two. "Hockley's artillery will be here in the center. These two beautiful cannon. You remember what we call them?" Several voices called out, "The Twin Sisters."

"That's right," I said. "And every time they fire, let's all give a cheer for the good citizens of Cincinnati who donated them to us. Let those girls rain down death and destruction with grapeshot or any shrapnel you stuff down their barrels. In fact, how about a cheer right now? A hearty cheer rang out.

The twin sisters will be supported on either side by four companies of infantry under Captain Henry Wax Karnes. Burleson's Volunteers will join Hockley on the left and Sherman's Second Volunteers Regiment will take on the right flank."

I turned to Seguin. "Juan, you will post your men with Lamar."

The men paused. Something extraordinary was about to happen. Sweat beaded a few foreheads, some nervously stroked their beards as the everyday sounds of the campground surrounded us. I looked up into each face. Schott was there, of course, and a goodly scattering of Joe's people. Juan led a substantial contingent of Mexicans. Mountain Man stood near the front, looking more ferocious than ever. I didn't see the Bounty Hunters, but it would not be surprising to lose them in such a crowd.

I knew all of us wondered if the other would be celebrating victory at the end of the day, or be cold carrion like the men at Goliad and the Alamo.

"Form your men up, but quietly. I want no shouting or firing until we meet the enemy."

Each nodded and left the tent. In short order I heard the men assembling outside the tent. I remained inside. I wished Emily were with me, and once again I drove any thought of her from my mind. I made a pledge for the umpteenth time that morning to honor her sacrifice any way I could.

"Don't worry, sweet girl. I'll kill the ignoble Napoleon of the West with my own hand."

There was a scratching at the tent flap. "General."

"Come in Deef."

"I saw her pantaloons. Well, I don't know it was hers, but there's a pair flapping in the wind. It's probably time to attack."

"The sentries?"

"From what I could see, some were nodding off. It looks like most of the camp is nodding off. If the general takes a siesta, the camp takes a siesta," he said, before adding, "Emily's done her job."

"Then it's time." I turned to walk out and caught my reflection in the mirror. The great Sam Houston, in need of a shave, stood tall in a fringe leather jacket over a filthy white ruffled shirt and blue breeches smudged with black clay mud. I could envision Santa Anna resplendent in a neatly pressed blue general's coat, bedazzled in ribbons and jeweled medals. A freshly starched white shirt, ruffles at throat and wrist. It was time to teach the eagle a few tricks.

"One thing, General. His tent is in the center, set back a bit, large and white. You might want to tell the men to be careful of it. You don't know where Emily's going to be."

I hadn't thought about that. "I thought you and her were enemies."

His brow furrowed, his eyes narrowed, and he sucked on his lips. "General. I told you she was a good soldier. A general takes care of his troops, is all."

I nodded, turned to leave and he rushed to hold the tent flap back.

I stepped into a sea of humanity. Normally there would be tinkling of weapons and tack as more than nine hundred men prepared to attack a camp twice their number. An occasional snort from a horse pawing for action punctured the quiet anticipation. Farmers wearing Sunday-go-meeting hats that had seen better days looked out from under their grimy Stetsons, steely-eyed, prepared to kill or be killed. Store clerks, some just arriving in their aprons, frontiersman in coonskin hats, dandies dressed more for the opera house than the battlefield, young boys about Zach's age, all stood quietly.

"Men, boys, soldiers, I am proud today to call you my brothers in arms, my comrades, Texicans all."

A cheer began, but I held up my hand. "Save our cheers for the victory. If we are to surprise the enemy, we must move silently."

The men lifted their muskets, but silently. Good. They were paying attention.

"We have toiled long and hard, and our long toil has been frustrating. But today, the frustration ends. Today, we have become a fighting force, and today we will fight."

Muskets lifted silently once more.

"We have the pepperbellies in a vice. Vince's Bridge is burned. They have no retreat. We will use stealth to cross that bayou" —I gestured toward the open space before us. "Emily's underwear on Santa Anna's tent poles tells us that neither he nor his troops are paying attention. We'll be on them before they know it.

"As we march into battle, keep in mind the cruelty of our enemy, the pain they have laid at our doorsteps. Remember the sacrifice of poor Zachary Schott. Remember the slaughter at Goliad. Remember the massacre at the sacred Mission La Bahía, and remember the brave martyrs at the Alamo. Our enemies showed no mercy to our comrades. Let us show them no mercy in turn. As we go forward, keep your eye on my sword. Trust in God and fear not. We go to conquer, and today, victory will be ours. Forward now."

We silently—as silent as clinking bridles and clanging canteens allowed—began our advance. The trees that offered shelter now seemed few and far between. The rise, which we hoped would cover our approach, seemed too slight to block out our advance. Lamar's cavalry had disappeared into the trees as he began the loop on the Mexicans' flank. The men pushed the Twin Sisters along on well-greased wheels. They crouched as low to the ground as a snake's belly. When they were only a few dozen yards away, I signaled for the Twin Sisters to be positioned. They were already loaded. I raised my sword, and when it dropped, the Sisters belched deadly shrapnel.

Hundreds of throats roared. "Remember the Alamo. Remember

Goliad." The cannon fired, then dropped to the ground, expecting a volley from the disoriented Mexicans, who had already begun to flee.

Then, as close to a roar as I could get. I called "Get up. Advance. The cowards are running." I spurred forward, urging the men to attack. Through the smoke and gunfire I heard a fife and drum corps I didn't even know we had strike up Yankee Doodle Dandy, a rather strange tune for the moment.

"Trust in God," I bellowed, "and fear not."

My voice thundered as the men quickly stood up, fired a second round, then charged after the retreating Mexicans. I felt my steed tremble and knew he had been hit. But like the fierce frontier beast he was, he kept going forward. A second strike. Then a third. The fourth brought him to his knees, and I started to ease out of the saddle. The fifth extinguished his extraordinary spirit as I leaped to the ground.

Around me churned the confusion and thunder. I grabbed the reins of a horse trotting by and pulled him to me. It was a Mexican's mount. Its silver trappings belied its bloody errand. I leapt to his back to gallop across the field of battle. My men were disappearing into the forest in hot pursuit, the names of Alamo and Goliad and an occasional Zach on their lips. It would be impossible to reign them in.

"Take prisoners like the Meskins do." Deef's voice rang as a clarion call to vengeance. I spotted Santa Anna's tent. No sooner did I spur the horse forward than a rifle ball shattered my ankle, wrapping my whole body in pain. With a whoosh of air, my second horse stumbled a step, then went down.

Deef appeared out of nowhere leading another Mexican mount. Yelling in pain, I leaned on him to stand, then he shoved me onto the mount. Each step sent lightning bolts into my ankle, but I had to get to Santa Anna's tent to make sure Emily was safe.

"You okay, General? I ain't through killing Meskins," Deef said.

Through gritted teeth, I called for restraint, but Deef would have none of that. "You just rest easy. I'll be back for you."

I cautiously eased the horse to Santa Anna's tent, dotted with rips and tears from grape shot and musket balls. My bowels seized when I visualized what I might find inside. Poking the horse's head into the tent, I gingerly entered. It was empty.

CHAPTER FORTY

In Santa Anna's Tent— San Jacinto

"We will begin here, Emily," Santa Anna said after sitting me at his table. "Draw a diagram of Houston's positions."

This would be a delicate business. I wanted to lie, but I was sure Santa Anna already knew much of the truth. But he didn't know all of it. How I wished I knew what parts of which he was ignorant. I proceeded with a general outline of the camp, as true a representation as I could. As I drew, Santa Anna had his private pour him a brandy. In my previous experience, not a usual thing for him at midday with a battle imminent. He drew his silver flask from inside his tunic and poured a few drops of a green liquid into the glass. Laudanum. Never had I seen him use it in daytime. This general had changed, and his change may explain the slack discipline I'd seen in the camp. How I wished I could get a message to Sam.

"I've been driving a wagon and tending to women most of the time," I said, "so I've seen a good deal of what's going on. Not all, but a good deal. Houston's been drilling his men, trying to get them into shape as if they're a real army. But mostly, they're just farmers and shopkeepers, not professional military like your troops."

"I know all this, Emily. Tell me something useful."

"They have artillery now," I said, "recently arrived. There are a pair of cannons called the "twin sisters" positioned here." I drew an "X." I was quite sure Santa Anna would already know this, but I hoped it had the air of confidentiality and would give some credibility to the lie that followed. "However, there are several other cannon that arrived earlier, disguised under blankets in farm wagons. They are concealed under bushes that have been cut and placed over them for camouflage. Right here." More "X's." His eyebrows raised. My first success.

"And the size of these guns?"

"*Lo siento,* Toño, I know nothing of these things."

He grabbed my wrist and twisted. "Don't lie to me, Emily. You have been sleeping with this man, known his every thought, and you tell me you don't know something so simple?"

I yelped, though in truth his grip did not hurt a great deal. I wanted to appear as much in his thrall as I could.

"Toño, please. He tells me nothing. It is one reason I am here. He uses me, throws me down like a used handkerchief only to pick me up again when he wants me. I thought when I left you, I would be running toward freedom and love. Instead, I found nothing but hardship and cruelty from the Indians, from Houston, from everyone else I met. I know he was tired of me and ready to sell me to the Apaches. I never understood how secure I was with you, how much you cared. Now that I've found my way back, I will do anything to stay, but I cannot tell you what I don't know."

He released my arm and softened his tone. "So, what else do you know?"

"First, please, allow me to discard these wet and filthy garments. No, don't call Isabella. One of your lovely silk robes will do for what follows." He smiled, had the private bring me the robe, then watched me change. I kept my back to him most of the time, occasionally allowing him a profile glimpse. Finally, I declined a brandy and sat with a glass of water while we continued the conversation.

"So if he is to move them forward, his men will have to pull them themselves. If you are able to breach him there, you might be able to defeat him entirely. Keep in mind, though, how little I know of military matters."

I knew there were plenty of mules to hitch to the cannon. Santa Anna would know so as well, but I hoped my declaration of ignorance would shield me.

His interrogation went on for over an hour. Finally, He seemed satisfied. I kissed his hand and embraced him. Thanked him again for giving me refuge, promised to serve him throughout what I knew would be a glorious triumph and reign over all of Mexico. It was what he wanted to hear, and his pride allowed him to believe it even from my lips, who had proved a traitor to him. I opened my robe and snuggled up to him.

"I am sure that with your skill and superior force, a well-planned attack will finish Houston," I said. "And I would love to be there to see him in chains."

We had lunch, then a session of lovemaking, or so one might call it in a sarcastic moment, for love had nothing to do with it. I was surprised to find both his endurance and his potency reduced. Afterwards, he dragged his rough hand over my cheek in a gesture he would probably have considered a caress, but by then I knew the true feel of such.

"We are an army which has covered great distances and accomplished much," he said. "For now, we will rest. Soon, we will attack, and the threat of this so-called republic and its renegade general will be finished."

And then, he fell asleep. Something I'd never seen him do in daylight. I took advantage of his slumber to retrieve my clothes and slip outside the tent, donning my blouse and skirt, damp and dirty though they both were. The slovenly troops made no attempt to stop me as I hung my undergarments on whatever limbs or tent poles were handy. The bloomers flapping in the breeze from the general's tent pole attracted the most attention in the form of pointing and smirks from whatever nearby troops happened to be awake. I hoped they would attract plenty of attention in the Texican camp as well.

Santa Anna was awakening as I re-entered the tent. He propped himself on an elbow, adjusted his silk nightshirt to cover his nether parts.

"Where have you been?"

"Answering a call of nature and hanging my laundry," I said.

"I should do the same," he said. "Not the laundry, of course. He pulled aside the curtain that separated our bed chamber from the rest of the tent.

"*Soldado,*" he called to his attendant. Then came the first cannon report, and we both heard the shell as it whizzed past the tent. "*Puta madre. ¿Que Pasó?*"

The General dashed out of the tent, unmindful of his attire, and I followed close behind. What I beheld amazed me. From Houston's camp I saw puffs of smoke from both cannon and rifles. A motley surge of troops, mounted and on foot forged through the swamps. Even at this distance we could hear the yells. Though we could distinguish no words, I knew that "Alamo" and "Goliad" figured among them, and I'm sure Santa Anna knew it, too. Bullets peppered the trees and bushes.

The general, barefoot, his skirts flapping about his knees called for his soldiers to grab their weapons and form ranks, but they ignored him, and began to run. Seeing that his efforts were useless, he ran back into his tent, me close behind him, and began stuffing a few papers into a leather case. Shouting orders to his attendant, who seemed not to know what to make of them, he dithered, grabbed a bottle of liquor, a quill, an inkwell, put down down the bottle and took up a wax seal instead. Santa Anna finally stuffed his bare feet into a pair of boots, seized a pistol and started out of the tent. I blocked his way.

"You can't go like this, Toño." I put a whimper in my voice. "It would be a disgrace for a man like you."

"I cannot wait, *Querida.*"

"I will not allow it." I turned to the attendant. "*Soldado,* remove your clothes." Looks of astonished puzzlement flew between the two men. "Now. The General will flee in your uniform undetected, for he must escape to lead the fight for Mexico on another day."

"*Pero, Señorita—*"

"*Basta, soldado.*" Santa Anna showed a flash of his customary authority. "Excellent notion, Emily. *Arriba. Arriba.*"

In short order, the soldier stood in his underwear, and my proud and rapacious general was reduced to the rank of private, though his silken nightshirt constituted finer underwear than any soldier ever hoped to wear. I wished I had more time to savor the moment.

"*Gracias,* Emily. *Hasta Luego.*"

With a kiss and a hug. He was gone. The private looked around the tent, then at me, then at the door, then back at me. It appeared he was waiting for an order, so I gave him one. "*Andale.*" He rushed through the door, and suddenly I was alone, though not really. The Texicans would be here shortly, and their bullets put me in as much danger as the Mexican army's. I wanted to head for cover, but dared not leave without a weapon.

Nothing around the General's table. There was a foot locker behind it, the padlock hasp lying open. Another measure of how lax Santa Anna had become. I threw it open and rummaged among the tunics and pants and epaulettes until my hand hit something metal.

I came up with a knife possessed of a very wide blade encased in a bloodstained leather sheath. The end of the steel handle was stamped with a "B." "Bowie?" It had to be. I pulled the weapon out and held it to the light. How many pepperbellies had this blade sliced open before its owner and inventor had finally succumbed? Well, maybe Emily West would find a few more. A savage thought that surprised me. Though not as much as the act that would follow before long.

I resheathed the knife, used one of the general's belts to strap it around my waist—not a bad fit once I punched in a new hole—I ran into the fray, keeping low to avoid the bullets that were flying everywhere. I didn't run far before I came on a scene that pulled me up short.

Joe Travis was surrounded by three men, two of them mounted, with pistols trained on him. The third walked toward him with a length of rope in his hand and a leer on his face.

"Got ourselves a live one now. Cash on the hoof."

I remembered well this trio of brothers—slavers all. Hard to forget the names—Zeke, Ike, and that original killer, Cain—though I didn't know which was which, it didn't much matter. Joe had been dodging them for weeks while training with the army, but now here they were, using the battle for cover to ply their vicious trade.

CHAPTER FORTY-ONE

The Prospect of Servitude

Looking back, my smartest route was obvious. Without my papers, I was as marketable as Joe, and what chance did I have against such as they and in such numbers? Prudence would have sent me looking for my general. But that's looking back.

In the moment, a fiery anger erupted in me—a fury at the men attacking Joe mixed with my rage against that other general. I suppose about twenty yards separated me from the group when I spotted them. I hastened my stride, not quite running, yelling as I came.

"Jim Bowie." Heads turned. "Jim Bowie's here."

The one with the rope in his hand spoke first. "It's that yeller bitch of Houston's."

I'd cut the distance in half by that time, and Joe took advantage of the distraction immediately. He dived under one of the horses and rolled free. Both horses began wheeling and prancing and tossing their heads. Joe leaped toward the gun hand of one of the men, now more engaged in trying to control his mount than in controlling Joe, who tore the man's pistol free and used it.

I heard the shots, but didn't have time to see the results because by that time I was face to face with the man holding the rope.

"What's this garbage about Jim Bowie?" He reached for his own gun, holstered at his hip.

I snarled, "He's right here." And I buried the blade in his gut.

He was the second man I'd killed, and this was much more personal than with the attacker from Santa Anna's army. That man had jumped me without a care to who I was. I'd fired, then been pulled away by someone else. It had been over in a second.

This man wanted me. In particular. And I felt the same about him. He hung on the blade for several long seconds, tried to reach for it, but lost his strength. He looked amazed, grunted, then fell away from me, clutching his stomach.

I wonder that I felt no revulsion or dismay to see his suffering, the blade dripping red in my hand. Instead, I felt triumph, pride, joy. When I recall it now, I feel just as triumphant, proud, and joyful.

He was still gasping and groaning when I wiped my blade on his shirt, resheathed the Bowie, and pulled the hogleg from its holster. Joe and I stood looking at one another over the bloody results of our work. He shook his head.

"My yellow rose. All that, and it only took a minute or so."

I stepped toward him, my arms wide. "Or maybe years," I whispered as we embraced.

***

We had a lot to talk about, Joe and I, but the battle was not over. The Mexicans had clearly lost, but the Texicans were still hungry for victims, probing bushes and groves and bayous for stragglers and fugitives. Bullets still zinged—not as thick and regular as before, but every one deadly nonetheless. We crouched next to a palo verde. He pulled a familiar-looking pouch from the inside pocket of his jacket.

"You were supposed to use that money to get out of here."

"I admit wasn't no sense to my staying. Wasn't no sense to my thinking I owed anyone nothing. But I still felt like a Texican somehow, and felt like maybe ... I can't explain it, Rose. I told you it don't make no sense."

"Well, you'll be a Texican slave now if you stick around here. Houston doesn't hold with servitude much, but he can't control everyone, so you'd best light out before another group like that one comes along."

"Here." He thrust the pouch at me.

"I said it's yours. It's yours."

"Ain't none of mine."

"Joe, you are one stubborn man and maybe not too bright on top of it." He continued to offer the pouch. I continued to not take it. "All right. No time for this argument. A split and no more conversation."

He smiled then and scooped a couple of handfuls of coin out of his pouch and stuffed them in his pockets. Then he handed the rest to me. I tied the pouch to my knife belt. This time it was Joe who stood and spread his arms. I was glad to step into them. "Maybe some time. Maybe not. But we been something together, ain't we, Rose?"

"Oh, indeed we have."

He sprinted to one of the dead slaver's horses, grabbed the other's bridle, and rode north toward a future as uncertain as any man's ever was. I stood watching him disappear into the tall grass, facing a future every bit as uncertain as his. But still and all, I'd always be his yellow rose. It was a sweet thought. Looking back, I'm pretty sure I was smiling.

CHAPTER FORTY-TWO

Aftermath

These boys meant it when they pledged no quarter. It was obvious within a matter of minutes that the enemy had been routed. Santa Anna had disappeared and hundreds, maybe thousands, of pepperbellies lay dead.

I urged my captured mount through the tent, calling Emily's name through gritted teeth, my ankle throbbing, but she was nowhere to be found. I felt my shirt jump, then my coat sleeve shudder as bullets buzzed through the canvas like so many swamp hornets. Deef came riding up.

"General, you've been wounded," he said, jumping off his horse to grab my torn boot, still in the stirrup which had kept it immobile. When he took it out of the stirrup, it felt like he had ripped my foot from my leg. I expected it to be gone when I looked down. Instead, I saw a piece of bone stuck poking through the leather. "We've got to get you to Dr. Stewart."

"Not until this is over."

"It is over, General. The boys are mopping up right now. This thing barely got started before it was over. We surprised them, and they never returned our first volley. They just started running."

"Ok, then, next thing is to get our men to fall back a bit. We don't want a slaughter. We're better than those murderers who shot down unarmed men. Tell them to stop the killing. I'll go find Dr. Stewart. He's supposed to be at the Y that leads to Vince's Crossing."

I heard a muffled gunshot in the distance.

"Me no Alamo," some Mexican cried out trying to save his worthless skin. They knew a special hell awaited the heartless victors at Goliad and the Alamo. Another bullet knocked fringe off my buckskin jacket.

"Let's go, fella." I urged the smallish mount forward, hanging onto the ornate silver saddle horn, inlaid with shining metal faces I did not know, but suspected them to be saints unique to the Mexican cavalry. They must have slept in today.

Human carnage is a trite phrase, but I don't know how else to describe what I was seeing. Mexican soldiers cried for help or their mothers as I rode out of the camp. Carcasses lay everywhere, thanks to the surprise attack provided by Emily's distraction. Few were able to stand and fight and those who did died immediately thanks to the original volley by my boys. The three hundred yards of bayou land held few Texican causalities.

The slavers lay together in a grove just off the road. At least these ignoble sons of the South had given their lives for a noble cause. I rode on amid the pungent smell of gunpowder and the rancid smell of blood and distant gunfire until I spied the fork that led to Vince's Ferry.

Another bullet grazed my rib cage and I felt an angry welt rising. "Damn."

My favorite George Washington story flashed through my mind. Always he was in front of his men, and always he came back to camp with his clothing torn by bullets, but his body unscathed. I hadn't been so lucky in founding Texas.

***

With Joe gone, I set out to find Houston or somebody who could tell me about his fate. I slogged through the bayou, dodging bullets as

Mexicans fell all around me. One boy barely in his teens lay dying. I stooped to hold his hand. His eyes flew open.

"Mamacita," he gasped, followed by a string of words I didn't understand.

"Sí." It was a soft answer, my heart breaking for his youth. He smiled through the pain, gave a great sigh that ended in bloody froth on his lips and his black eyes dulled. I closed them.

A cannon ball exploded, knocking down century-old cedar trees. Flying wood peppered me, not close enough to harm me, but enough to send me plunging back into the mire and muck.

***

Dr. Stewart was ready as he could be when I got there. Him and ol' John Barley Corn were on intimate terms.

"I didn't figure you'd get yourself all shot up," he said, offering his small frame as a brace to ease me off my third horse. "Get me two men over here." His voice strained with the effort of bearing my weight.

Ryan, the brother of poor Zach, that youngster who had got us all yelling 'Remember the Alamo' came running up, bullets still flying all around him.

"My…my Pa got shot. I'm helping with him. 'Sides, them Mexicans are on the run," he said.

"How bad's your Pa?"

"Just his shoulder. Grapeshot went through and through, the doc says." I looked over at Schott, propped up on a wagon wheel. He waved weakly. Ryan grunted as he took my weight off Dr. Stewart. Slightly built though he was, he was all ready to do a man's work. This new nation was going to need lads like him.

"Thank you, boy. When you're done here, get back to your Pa. Make sure you take him home."

Dr. Stewart spread a quilt under a big oak, and another man joined Ryan to help me hobble to the makeshift bed, and the doc fluffed a couple of feather pillows against the trunk so I could sit upright. He brought out a knife and stooped to start cutting the boot off my foot, stopping to take a swig out of a silver flask decorated with gold.

"How about me? I'm in need of something to help control this pain." He held the flask out to me.

"Doc. We need help right now." The call came from a few yards away. I looked up to see a burly farmer clutching his belly, blood spurting.

"He needs you more than I do. Go."

"He can wait. You're the general."

"What about Santa Anna? Has he been captured?" A chorus of "No's" and negative head shakes greeted that question.

I closed my eyes to visualize the glorious moment he would be brought before me, resplendent in his gold-braided general's uniform dotted with medals, hat in hand, his bicorn wavering, on his knees begging for his life. I pictured his brow furrowed, his eyes shining in fear, tears wetting his swarthy face. Let him feel some of the helpless anguish he'd visited on Emily, when all she had left to hope for was a measure of human dignity denied her just as it was the brave soldiers at the Alamo and La Bahía. Faintly I heard the bugle cry of No Quarter. That's what I would do when I executed him. I'd have the bugler play the chilling No Quarter as Santa Anna was dispatched to his master, the devil. While they were being killed for being the enemy I had to remember that the soldados deserved some mercy. Many were young boys just following orders. Santa Anna was another matter. He was the force of evil.

"General. Sir."

I looked up. "What?"

"We done won it." It was a farmer in overhauls, bearded, homespun one-piece gray shirt I suspected was once white, felt hat sporting an eagle feather, clamped down over a bandage. A chorus of voices joined in. "Yessir, we did it." All the men had various injuries, enough to keep them away from the slaughter I could still hear filtered through the woods.

Deef had declared victory and now this farmer, fresh from a battle only minutes old, confirmed it. From my vantage point I had to agree with them, but it wouldn't be complete until Santa Anna stood before me, captured and capitulating.

"Anyone here know Juan Seguin?"

"*Sí*, senior, he's my cousin." His clothing was a little more expensive than the others, although his white shirt had been ruined by blood and his arm was in a sling.

"Find Juan and anyone else in charge of men. Tell them from me to stop the slaughter. We want captives, not corpses. We're not savages. We don't kill for revenge, or for the fun of killing."

Given my recent imaginings, though, I wasn't quite sure I'd be able to follow my own orders when I came face-to-face with the Napoleon of the West.

***

I spotted Sam from a rise just outside the bayou. He sat beneath a big oak tree, his face twisted in pain, his left leg stretched out before him, Dr. Stewart working on him. They were surrounded by a group of men too awed to touch the legendary leader. I lifted my skirts to run toward him, anxious to discover his condition and do what I could to help.

***

"Let go of me." Emily's voice broke my reverie. I opened my eyes to see her held back by the farmer who had proclaimed victory. He was holding her forearm with his good arm, and she held his bad arm in a vice. Considering his battle wounds, I figured Emily could have flipped him had she wanted.

"You ain't going nowhere, Missy. If the general wants your attention, he'll call for it."

"I need to attend to him." She pushed to move him aside, but he shoved back, and she stumbled backward.

"You may be a house nigger, but you're still a slave."

Slave or not, her color and lack of proof to the contrary had branded her as surely as if she wore an "S" on her forehead. I knew the thought terrified her, but she carried on as if it didn't matter. I vowed once more to make sure she didn't fall into bondage. She looked at me, eyes both defiant and pleading.

I waved my arm and called, "Let her through."

"Well, okay," the soldier said. "If the general wants you." He stood aside, and Emily rushed to me.

That soldier had no idea how much I wanted her at the moment. It would be special for her to be here to see me pass judgment and order Santa Anna's execution. Only the two of us would understand her special justice.

She yanked her arm free with a glare born of years of frustration and started toward me. I couldn't help but notice the appreciative stare the frontiersman had for her receding form. My glare stopped that.

She bent over, her lips barely moving. "Sam is that your only wound?"

I chuckled, in spite of the pain, "I think it's enough."

"You know what I mean."

"I do, Sweetness. There's a minor graze my rib cage on the right, but it's more of a nuisance, and I'm glad to have you tend it instead of that drunken butcher."

***

A bullet had shattered his ankle, and it was apparent that the doctor in charge was so far into his cups that he was bound to do more harm than good. No one else had the courage to take charge of the situation, so I began ministering to the wound myself. The so-called doctor, working across the way, would be particularly outraged when he learned I had commandeered his precious flask and used the contents to cleanse the wound.

What did I know about doctoring? Not a thing beyond what I'd picked up by observing and listening here and there, and I was terrified. Here was a great man and the fate of a new nation at stake, but no one else stepped forward. Even know-it-all Deef Smith stood there trying to look tough and vigilant against rogue attacks from the defeated Mexicans, but I could tell he was limp and useless in face of the real crisis.

***

Emily offered the flask. I took a long pull; not the smooth Tennessee sipping whiskey I was used to, but the sharp breath-catching corn liquor that probably was in Doc's private and portable still that morning.

When I coughed, pain shook me. She looked up. "Does the Doc have laudanum?"

I shook my head. The last thing I needed right then was Oriental opiates. They might make me think we were losing instead of mopping up what remained of a once-proud army. I'd make do with home-made brew rather than a flight of fancy, until I knew exactly what was going on, and that would probably take a few hours.

I could still hear faint shots as the battle flowed down the road to Vince's Ferry, now destroyed, or beyond the Mexican camp where the land turned into swamp.

"Damn, Sweetness. Give me another swig of the rot-gut or go easy on my ankle."

"Don't be a milksop. There are plenty of men hurt worse than this." But she flipped it to me anyhow. The crowd grew larger as wounded came to the oak tree. Other men were herding captives in front of them. A few of the wounded men found a new mission in guarding me, standing erect, arms in slings, and those who couldn't stand found barrels and trees to sit on or lean against. Maybe I was being a milksop.

"Well, someone give me a battle report," I moaned and yanked my ankle away from her as she got the last of the boot off. I looked down to see a sorry mess, bone sticking out, bloody flesh and my foot angled in a queer direction. Even to my inexperienced eye I knew it needed splinting and possibly surgery, perhaps amputation. No. I refused to consider that.

Emily continued to work her way over my body, poking her fingers into bullet holes in my clothing, feeling for injuries I might not know I had. A couple of times I felt a sweet caress and a loving pat.

"You must be one of God's favorites," she whispered, poking a finger through a hole in my jacket right over my heart. "There's bullet holes everywhere."

Once she reached my head, she grinned, then lightly knocked on it. "Bad luck for your ankle, if you'd been shot here, the bullet'd bounced off."

In spite of my pain I couldn't help but chuckle. Then she got down to business with my ankle. I could barely feel her touch, whether she was so gentle or the wound had gone numb. She mumbled to herself as she studied the ankle.

I figured if I kept talking, it might take my mind off the pain, and I did have important business to tend to.

"Do you know where Santa Anna is? He escaped his tent. I went in there looking for you. . ." I let the meaning hang. "You were. . ." A fresh throb of pain shot up my leg and into my head. "…gone," I finished through gritted teeth.

"The coward's dressed as a private," she chuckled. "He did go dashing out in his silk nightshirt at first. I helped him throw his private's uniform over the nightshift. Then he ran like a scalded cat."

"You were a soldier today, Sweetness." She gave me a warning look to hear the endearing name called so loud. "I don't care who hears me, Sweetness. I can call the bravest warrior on the battlefield anything I want. Without your sacrifice, this victory would have been impossible. I'm very sorry you had to do it."

She nodded, tears scalding her cheeks. "I did it…for…you…for freedom." She fell silent, devoting herself to the task at hand. "We'll talk later."

***

I summoned the help of three men brave enough to hold down the Houston's leg while I set about what seemed the most urgent task—clearing the bone chips from the wound. To my unprofessional eyes, it seemed likely they'd cause infection if left to themselves.

The general moaned and cursed the while. Voices from the crowd yelled at me, the "uppity slave," the "nigger whore," to stop, and my heart tore to cause him such pain. However, no one tried to pull me loose. If they did, they'd have had to take over, and I guess that idea of becoming responsible for the health of the general terrified them more than anything else.

I kept telling myself what I was doing was right in order to silence the fearful voice inside me that wanted me to stop. Here was the man I cared for over all others on earth, and I was conflicted because I was causing pain so I could save him. Maybe my prideful heart had finally soared beyond its bounds. I could be destroying or crippling the founder of a nation before the nation even began.

What kept me going more than anything else while I went about my probing was the general's incessant calling for information. I told him about Santa Anna. He instructed Deef to tell the others what to look for as they searched. His faithful friend left immediately and I wished I could have gone with him.

Sam called me a brave soldier. I'd have kissed him if I could.

For some reason, the salty taste of the tears that trickled down my cheeks onto my lips helped me to concentrate on the tedious work. Finally, I could find nothing more to remove from the wound. It needed a final cleansing.

"Be quiet, General. This is going to hurt, so be brave. Your men are watching."

***

She poured Doc's raw whiskey over the wound, I might as well have been molten lava the way it burned. A moan slipped from my lips. Sweetness grabbed my hand to squeeze tight. She started to hug me, then stopped. I could tell she felt dozens of eyes probing her slightest move. "Hold still, General. I'm nearly finished."

A murmur started among the men and turned into an inferno of hate. Emily looked up and her eyes widened. Comments rained down from the crowd.

"Ya ain't so tough now, you pepperbelly."

"Ain't you got no respect? He's the head *jalapeño.*"

Kill 'im now. Gut 'im like a side of beef. Use a Bowie knife on 'im. He ain't worth a bullet."

The men parted and there stood the disheveled Napoleon of the West, a grinning Deef Smith by his side. Santa Anna wore the simple white canvas uniform of a dragoon private, just as Emily had said.

"I am Antonio de Padua María Severino López de Santa Anna y Pérez de Lebrón," he said. "I am here to negotiate the terms of surrender."

Whatever else you could say about him, he didn't lack for gall. An image of Emily and that coward together flashed through my mind, and my hand felt for my pistol, but it turned out Emily got first crack at him. And who had a better right? She stepped toward him. They stared at one another for a moment.

"Toño." She acknowledged him

He acknowledged her with a slight nod of his head. "So, my little yellow rose, we meet again" His tone was bitter, his eyes brimming with fury.

For a moment the throbbing in my ankle was replaced by a thunderbolt of jealousy. Here stood the man who had raped her, yet he calmly addressed her as if they'd just met on a Sunday picnic after mass.

Emily said nothing for a moment, then she balled up her fist and whacked him in the beak. Drew blood, too, and she wasn't finished yet. That pretty knee I'd adored so many times suddenly became a weapon and the great man went to his knees, hands grabbing his crotch. Seeing him humiliated like that drew cheers from the crowd and got my warrior blood flowing.

Humiliated by a woman and splayed on his knees before the very men his army had tried to kill, it was time to pass sentence.

"Here's my terms of surrender, you pepperbelly pretender. Your army's ours to either join the republic or get back to Mexico. As for you, better say your prayers because the firing squad will be waiting at dawn."

More cheers. Then a banshee-like "Noooo" cut through it all. Her soft touch stayed my hand like iron manacles. Her ethereal whisper floated into my ear. She was on her knees, like a supplicant in church.

"How many times you said you wouldn't act like this beast disguised as a general. How many times you said Texas will be different."

Tears ran down her cheek. "Don't miss your chance to prove it."

And like the voice of the Almighty, she called me to my better self.

How was I to fight the will of the woman I loved? Who had just invoked the Creator himself? Yet, here was the man who had destroyed the Alamo, who was responsible for the murders in Goliad. It would only take a small flicker of my hand and Deef Smith would dispatch him right now. Emily's hand felt like manacles and her prayerful voice destroyed my burning desire for revenge—for the dead men, and for her. I drew slow breaths to calm myself as the men stared intently, awaiting my final verdict. I hoped my voice would be steady and strong.

"You carry a lot of names with you, General, but I'm just plain ol' Samuel Houston." I inclined my head to encompass the gathering mass of men. "And these are frontiersmen and farmers and clerks and young boys—even a woman dressed as a man—and God only knows who else, that defeated you."

"Any of these men would gladly execute you for what happened at La Bahía, in Goliad and at the Alamo and for the miserable days in pouring rain and snow and cold we spent preparing for battle while most of South Texas fled your army. You kept all of them wet, miserable, and sick. I would wield the sword of justice myself, but right now you're more help alive than dead, so I'm not going to order up a firing squad after all."

A hush fell over the men. In the distance, amid the sounds of war— gunfire, the boom of a cannon, and men ordering their captives— a mockingbird sang her song.

I held up my hand. "Do you hear that?" The men looked at each other. "Listen closely." I could see them strain, some with eyes closed others with veins sticking out of their necks, heads cocked, so intently did they listen."

"It might even be an angel's song."

Finally, Ryan's voice: "I hear a mockingbird singing."

"You're right, Ryan. A mockingbird. One of God's own creatures, bringing a peaceful song into this devastation. Maybe it's time for mercy. We have what we want. The freedom to listen to the mockingbird each morning when we awaken. Is there anything greater than the smell of the fresh turned earth of your own land, the sound of commerce in the city and the right to raise your children to be greater than you are? Maybe it's time for mercy."

A few of the men shook their heads negative, but most of the men were nodding. I turned to Santa Anna.

"Here are my non-negotiable terms. You are to write a dispatch to your officers telling them this is over. I want that dispatch to order them to join us or go home. I'll free you once Texas is free of them."

I turned to the men. "You did it. You just established a nation."

Again, a roar of approval.

I felt tears tug at me. The men had won the battle, but a black woman most of them considered a slave, had sacrificed her dignity to help them to victory. I put my other hand over Emily's restraining hand.

"But you wielded the sword of victory," I whispered before returning to my address of the men.

***

The general made a speech I barely heard, so relieved was I that he'd agreed not to execute Santa Anna. Yet I was lost in my own confusion. Why would I feel that way about a man who had been so brutal to me? A question I cannot answer to this day. I emerged from my turmoil in time to hear Houston's final commands concerning his opponent.

"Gentlemen, convey the general to a wagon. Make sure he is securely bound and guarded by three men around the clock. Make sure he's fed and watered. We'll deal with him in a more civilized manner than he treated us because we're better than he is. We are Texans. Fearsome in battle, merciful in victory."

There was grumbling. "Listen. Listen to me. We are no longer Texicans, a mixed breed. We are Texans."

"Texans for Texas." He raised a fist.

Deef Smith stepped forward, his rifle held high. "Texas."

The grumbling turned to cheers, and Santa Anna was led away.

I hoped my whisper carried over the cheers. "Of all your heroic deeds today, General, that stands above them all."

CHAPTER FORTY-THREE

Dragon's Teeth

When the cheering died down and the men turned to preparing to return home, Emily showed me a small handful of bloody fragments.

"These used to be part of your ankle, General. What should I do with them?"

Greek mythology seemed appropriate in this moment of victory.

"Just like Cadmus sowed dragons' teeth that built up a great city, these are the seeds of our new republic."

She cocked her head, quizzical.

"In Greek mythology, the city of Thebes was founded by sowing dragon's teeth."

She grinned. "You are a sentimental man, General, and that's a wonderful idea."

She turned to Deef Smith. "Mr. Smith, would you do the honors?"

"I don't take no orders from—"

"Stop it Deef!"

The fact that I could roar in my condition startled everyone. Smith jumped to attention. "You told me she's a good soldier. You were even worried she'd be caught in the crossfire."

"But General. . ." He paused, looking down, his face reddening.

Emily extended the palm of her hand on which lay the seeds of a nation, at least according to my mythology.

"Not an order. A request." A pause. "Please."

Not a word from Deef, but he took them and set about jabbing the earth with his knife to make a planting trench.

CHAPTER FORTY-FOUR

The Best Medicine

We managed to salvage a few boards from one of the carts the soldiers had abandoned. It took some doing to line up the bones, and I was not at all certain we were doing it right. At last, though, the leg was splinted, bound, stable. I knelt beside him. "It's the best we can do till I get you to a real doctor."

He was still breathing very hard, groaning occasionally, and his "Thank you, Sweetness," sounded nothing like the hearty voice I was so used to. I wiped his brow.

CHAPTER FORTY-FIVE

That Letter Home

For the third morning in a row, Mother, I'm on the veranda of Morgan's Hotel, looking over the calm waters of Galveston Bay and I believe I've finally brought you up to date on my adventures. However, this letter has grown to so many pages, that I despair of mailing it. Between the bulk of it and the unreliability of the mails in these parts, I think it would be better to read it aloud to you before our fire when I return, which I trust will be soon.

I had meant to finish yesterday, but the General interrupted me with a call to supper. I know you're wondering about the General and me. All I can say at this point is that I am wondering as well. It will be a matter to relate in person, I think, not in a letter.

With all my love and in hopes that we will embrace anon.

Emily

"Still on that letter to your mother?"
"Your timing is good, General, I just finished."
Houston hopped on his good leg into a position where he could sit

on the chair beside me. I'd have helped him, but he'd have forbidden it even though he occasionally slipped and sprawled. I nodded.

"Must have told her everything by now, huh?" He winked and smiled. A warm breeze ruffled the pages in my lap.

I shook my head. "No, General. Not everything. Not quite." I passed on a wink and smile of my own, and we settled down to watch the pelicans sail over the still waters.

My soul was at peace as I studied his face from time to time, placid, as if he had no worry in the world. He reached over to wrap my hand in his. My heart thundered. He was becoming bold about these public displays, which carried risk for both of us. For my own reputation as a single woman of color and for his as the soon-to-be president of a new nation.

He released my hand and reached into his inside coat pocket. "You might have to add a little postscript to that letter," he said. He handed me a leather wallet, tied with a rawhide thong.

"What's this?" I said. I started to unwrap the thong. He held his palm up. "No need, Emily. It's what you've been waiting for. Your papers proving you're a free woman. If they're ever questioned, you can send the varlet to me or to Andy Jackson himself, who will shortly receive notice of your heroism. Plus some back wages that Jim Morgan owed you."

"But I thought he went back to New York."

"He'll pay me back eventually." He looked at me sideways, waiting for my reaction. I hugged the packet to my breast, stifled a sob. I closed my eyes and struggled for control, for I saw again the flames in Santa Anna's tent, gazed on the black powder they left after they'd consumed that contract, that fragile safeguard to my freedom. Once again my skin burned as if the fire enveloped me. Once again, my heart froze to gaze on the ashes.

"What's the matter, Sweetness? Aren't you happy?"

Sam's voice called me back to the present, and the heat I felt at that moment had nothing to do with pain, suffering, or fear. Only gratitude and the impulse to give unto him as he had given unto me.

"I thought that might be worth a kiss, at least."

I pressed his hand to my cheek and whispered. "You've earned a lot more than a kiss, General." He started to rise. "Just not here and now."

"Okay, then." He smiled and settled back. We watched the still waters together for a while. He drank deeply from a flask. Offered it to me. I shook my head.

"Later, maybe."

More silence.

"I'll be going to N'Orleans for treatment to my ankle."

More silence. I knew what was coming next, and I'd been both hungering for it and dreading it.

"Will you go with me?"

Again, my heart thundered. There had been too many slurs against him because of me. Sometimes there were taunts when we went out to dinner. I kept figuring out ways to dine in his room. And I had become nearly as apprehensive about his increasing devotion to demon rum as about the catty remarks.

"As my wife."

Oh, dear. It wasn't the first time he had proposed, some I felt owed more to alcohol than to affection. I could tell by his bearing and speech that this was not one of those.

"Sam, the sentiment against us is so strong ... " I looked around fearful of spies and eavesdroppers. He stomped his crutch on the floor and rose to his feet.

"I don't give a tinker's dam about sentiment." His voice rose. "Hey, everybody, listen up. I love this woman and she's going to be Mrs. Samuel Houston."

I looked around. There was no "everybody." Just us. The way a proposal ought to be done. My heart suddenly calmed.

"Yes, Sam, I'll marry you." He grabbed me for a promise kiss to seal the deal. I kissed him like I'd never shared a kiss with him ever before.

Farewell

I t was dawn when I slipped out of the bed Sam and I had tossed around like a summer storm. He still snored softly. I snatched quill and paper from the writing desk and began my note:

My dearest General,

You have my heart and always will have. I trust I've proved that a thousand times in a thousand ways, but I confess to a certain duplicity when I accepted your proposal last evening. I will forever be your wife in my own eyes, and, I hope, in God's. I know what I'm about to write is not a description of the "new us" I toasted the other morning, but I know upon reflection you'll realize the truth of my words when I tell you the world will never accept us. For all your warrior toughness, you have a naiveté about such matters, assuming that your energy and optimism will bring everyone else along with you. Most of the time, it works, even against great odds. But you can never know the bitter reality of rejection and suspicion that falls automatically upon those of us who belong to the lower races.

Perhaps in another place, another time our love could

be consummated.

Texas is too big, important—you are too important—to risk even for our love, which is as true as any since Eden.

I leave the money along with my note, since I still have enough from my earlier savings to carry me back to my mother, which is, when all is said and done, where I belong.

Please do us both proud as you go on building your own legend and that of your new nation.

Yours with love, longing, and regret.

Emily

HISTORICAL CHARACTERS IN *THE YELLOW ROSE*

Emily West/Morgan

Emily West was widely believed to share the last name of her employer, the entrepreneur James Morgan. There is even an Emily Morgan Hotel in downtown San Antonio. However, the belief about her last name was was apparently born of the common assumption of the time and place that colored people were slaves to their employers and thus bore their corresponding surnames. You wouldn't give your horse or dog a last name, after all.

In fact, Emily was, as we've presented her in *The Yellow Rose,* a free black woman. She was born in New Haven, Connecticut and was residing somewhere in New York's Hudson Valley when she signed a contract with Morgan committing herself for a period of one year as a housekeeper in his New Washington's Association Hotel. Morgan was to pay her $100 and provide transportation to Galveston Bay on board the company's Schooner.

Here are facsimiles of her signature and of Morgan's on the contract.

The matters of her relationship with Houston and her legendary dalliance with Santa Anna at San Jacinto in *The Yellow Rose* are a mix of of our invention and popular myth. We also invented her relationship with her mother and their dream of starting an inn. It is possible that she and her mother both worked for Morgan and lived in his house in the Hudson Valley. However, that, like so much else about her life, is speculation. All efforts to trace her whereabouts following the revolution have failed. In some ways it is fitting that her fame is tied entirely to the time she spent in Texas.

Sam Houston

Sam became first president of the Texas Republic and served two terms. When Texas joined the union in 1845, he became one of her first senators and served until 1860. His Waterloo with his fellow Texans came at the onset of the Civil War when he refused to pledge his allegiance to the Confederacy, largely over his opposition to slavery. His principled stand in the matter was a contradiction, since he owned slaves himself. *The Yellow Rose* is true to his internal conflict in that regard. He retired from politics soon after the war began and died in 1863.

Along the way, in 1840, he married Margaret Lea, who helped to eventually convert him from Catholic to Baptist. He also, most amazingly, took a vow of abstinence, which he mostly kept until the end of his life. The site of his 1854 baptism is an official Texas Historical Site on Rocky Creek with the charming address of Farm to Market Road 50 at Sam Houston Road.

Erastus "Deaf" (usually pronounced "Deef") Smith

Smith was a master spy and gatherer of intelligence. He was pivotal in both these roles and as a messenger during the revolution. Among other deeds, just as in *The Yellow Rose*, he carried Travis' message from the Alamo to Gonzales and shepherded Susan Dickinson to Sam after the massacre.

Following San Jacinto, he gathered a company of Texas Rangers and led important raids against Mexican soldiers.

He retired from the military soon after and died in 1837 at the age of fifty. We have not been able to track down cause of death, but there is no mention of a battlefield injury.

General Antonio Lopez de Santa Anna

Santa Anna rose through the military and political ranks during Mexico's struggle against Spain in the early nineteenth century. Mexico achieved independence in 1821, and by 1834 he had abolished the new constitution of 1824, substituted his own "seven laws," and become dictator.

His early victories in the Texas Revolution—The Alamo and Goliad, for example—proved pyrrhic as his supply lines stretched thin, and bad weather outstripped the capacity of his troops' uniforms to keep them warm. By the time he reached San Jacinto, Santa Anna was leading a hungry, cold and demoralized force. Houston's "Runaway Scrape" strategy was vindicated.

After San Jacinto, Santa Anna and President Burnet signed the Treaty of Velasco, ceding Mexico's claim to the territory appropriated by the Texans. He was granted safe passage back to Veracruz, where he reentered Mexican military and political life. He made repeated attempts to take power, suffered several banishments to such places as Jamaica, Cuba, and New York. All his tries to re-establish his dictatorship came to naught. He died in Mexico city in 1876 at age 82.

An interesting sidelight on the life of "The Napoleon of the West" concerns his wooden leg. His left leg was amputated after a battle against the French in 1838 (He ordered it buried with full military honors.), and a prosthetic of cork and wood replaced it. That leg was, in turn, captured during the 1846-1848 Mexican-American conflict and is on display at the Military museum in Springfield, Illinois. I was once privileged to to view its subsequent replacement in the Mexican National Museum in Mexico City. I had no idea it was anywhere near till my eyes lighted suddenly on its privileged space in the display case.

It's a fine artifact. However, Bob and I are glad that neither we nor Emily had to deal with it.

A SPECIAL TRIBUTE TO MY LATE FRIEND AND CO-AUTHOR, BOB STEWART

Bob Stewart died on Nov. 16, 2014, not long after he and I finished *The Yellow Rose.* Our writing partnership began with an introduction from a mutual friend and writer, Les Edgerton. He thought we'd get along, and how right he was. We were an unlikely combination—a California guy whose views on religion and politics hardly matched up with those of the staunch Texas conservative Christian that Bob was. The fact that we were able to join forces at his invitation to complete this novel testifies to the professionalism and humanity that defined his character. Solidly devoted to conservative values though he was, he wrote with passion, romance, and a healthy dose of progressive thinking. The fact that we were able to make a team testifies to the notion that differing views don't necessarily create mutual hostility.

I close with an epitaph that Bob himself liked to quote:

Texan born
Texan bred
When I'm gone
I'll be Texan dead

ABOUT THE AUTHOR

Carl Brush has been writing since he could write, which is quite a long time now. He grew up and lives in Northern California, close to the roots of the people and action of most of his historical novels—*The Maxwell Vendetta*, its sequels, *The Second Vendetta*, and *Swindle in Sawtooth Valley*. *Bonita* and its sequel, *Bonita's Quest* are Brush's fourth and fifth novels of early California. *The Yellow Rose* adds one more to the list of works for both Brush and Stewart.